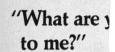

"What are y...
to me?"

Rynn's voice was hoarse and he sucked in his breath as Maressa's fingers slid across his warm chest, lightly grazing his nipples.

"I'm trying to get you to stay here," she murmured, continuing her exploration of his muscled torso.

"Be sensible, Maressa. How would it look, my strolling out of your place tomorrow morning?" he reasoned, but his breathing was becoming irregular.

"Sensible is not what I'm in the market for right now." She smiled seductively. Leaning over, she traced the line of his neck with her tongue, ending at the sensitive spot behind his ear.

Rynn muttered something unintelligible. Then his arms went around her tightly, and his weight pressed her against the bed....

THE AUTHOR

Living in Texas with her husband, a marriage therapist, and their young daughter, Kristin James makes time to read as much as possible and to indulge her yen for travel. She has also managed to have over a dozen successful books published since 1978, the year after she obtained her law degree.

Romance readers will also know this talented and prolific author as Lisa Gregory or Sharon Stephens. It was Kristin's lifelong love of writing that led her to become a full-time writer, and for that she credits her parents, both of whom were in the newspaper business.

A Wedding Gift

KRISTIN JAMES

Harlequin Books

TORONTO • NEW YORK • LONDON
AMSTERDAM • PARIS • SYDNEY • HAMBURG
STOCKHOLM • ATHENS • TOKYO • MILAN

Published June 1985

ISBN 0-373-25162-9

Printed in Canada

MARESSA SCOTT perched on a counter of the set, legs folded Indian fashion under her. The set was pushed into one corner of the studio, as it always was, except when her cooking show was being taped. The L-shaped arrangement of a mock stove, sink and nonworking refrigerator was shoved against the wall. The kitchen island on which she did all her food preparation lay on its side atop the stove. The low round table and the two chairs used in the interview portion were fitted into the angle of the L. Seen like this, the whole set looked cheap and flimsy, which it was. The magic of television cameras would transform it into a sparkling, modern kitchen.

Maressa chewed on her pencil and studied the woman across from her. Lynn Cawper produced the syndicated cooking show "Maressa's Kitchen," as well as several other weekly shows. She sat with her feet propped on a second folding chair, ankles crossed. She was reviewing Maressa's plans for the show, which was to be filmed in two days. As usual, a faint frown creased her forehead. Maressa had given up trying to figure out what the frown meant. As far as she could tell, it had nothing to do with whether Lynn liked the material.

She rarely disapproved of something Maressa had planned. Her scripts were almost always perfectly timed, interesting and slightly humorous. That wry touch of humor was one of the things that had made "Maressa's Kitchen" so popular. Lynn glanced up and smiled, erasing the line of worry between her eyes. "It looks great. I wish they were all this easy."

"Thank you." Maressa leaned back on her hands. "As long as I can keep Mrs. Greenwald from clamming up on me, I think it will be a good show."

"You'll manage," Lynn assured her, putting a cigarette between her lips and lighting it. "You always do. Even with someone like that pipsqueak who could hardly get out a word to me."

Maressa chuckled. "Harris McMillan? He is a little shy, but he's an absolute whiz at making cheesecake."

Lynn shrugged. "Whatever turns you on." She drew in a breath of smoke and blew it out slowly, tilting back her head. "Whew! What a week. You been busy with the wedding?"

Maressa nodded. Her younger brother, Kenyon, was getting married in a few days, and Maressa was to make the ornate wedding cake. The girl Kenyon was marrying, though very sweet, was young and indecisive. As it turned out, Maressa and her sister Annie had taken on most of the responsibility for getting the wedding done correctly and on time. Maressa had hired the caterers and the florists and booked the reception hall, and Annie had assumed the duties involving the invitations, dresses and the church. It didn't surprise Maressa when she found herself delegated to a position of command in the proceedings; being the most levelheaded member of her artistic family, she was always the one who got things done. Still, it bothered her slightly that Denise, Ken's bride, was so willing to let another woman run her wedding. How would the girl manage Ken, who could be hardheaded and domineering at times? Would she meekly go along with whatever he decided to do? Considering some of Ken's past schemes, Maressa sincerely hoped she would not.

"I certainly have," Maressa answered Lynn's question, turning her mind away from Denise's possible marital problems. "Everything's in a mess, of course. I have to meet Denise at the bakery in a few minutes to choose the style of her wedding cake."

"Funny," Lynn commented. "I never expected your brother to get married as soon as he got out of college. He's always seemed so wrapped up in his career."

"Oh, he still is. Getting married won't change that. I think Ken's wife will always have to put up with the fact that acting comes first with him."

Lynn raised her eyebrows. "Does the girl know that?"

Maressa shrugged. "If she knows Ken at all, she must have figured it out." Maressa frowned and continued thoughtfully, "Although...they've known each other such a short time, this play Ken's doing now is the first one he's been in since they met. But the theater is all he ever talks about."

Lynn grinned wickedly. "Most men I know don't

do a lot of talking when they're giving a girl the rush."

Maressa chuckled in agreement. "And did he ever give her a rush! You know Ken—he's so theatrical. He met Denise in a sophomore history course that he had to make up so he could graduate. She lent him her notes one day, and after that he started sending her flowers and showing up at her dorm with a book of poetry in his hand. All the classic romantic things. They've only known each other for three months, but they've hardly been apart the whole time. Why, I don't think he's spent more than one evening with all his old cronies since they started dating."

"Maybe he's changed."

"Ken? Don't count on it. It's just that he went about falling in love with his usual single-minded compulsiveness. So he saw, heard and thought of nothing but Denise. He wanted to be around only her. But pretty soon he'll start wanting to include all his friends in their life. He can't stand to be without a crowd for long."

Lynn smiled and shook her head in amusement. "So how's Elizabeth taking it?"

"Mother? She's the eye of the hurricane, what else? She's locked in her study with a new book, perfectly oblivious to Ken's nerves or Annie's and my running around. But after the wedding, she'll heave a great sigh and say, 'Well, thank heavens that's over. Maybe now I'll be able to get some rest.'"

Lynn laughed. She had once interviewed Elizabeth Gaither for her noonday show and had found her both as maddening and delightful, as most people did. "You know, that show your mother did was such a success that I've been thinking of asking your stepfather to be on one day."

"Lionel?" Maressa raised her eyebrows in doubt. "He's unusual, of course, but...well, he's not as talkative as Mother. He's shy and introverted. I'm not sure you could get him to say a thing."

"Too bad." Lynn shrugged her shoulders. "It isn't every day you meet someone who designs toys for a living."

"That's true." Maressa smiled and jumped lithely off the counter. She was a tall, slender young woman who looked good on television. When taping her show, she wore neat, fashionable dresses, but today she had dressed casually in faded jeans, a bright blue halter top that left her shoulders and much of her back bare and leather sandals. She wore no makeup, and the pale golden freckles sprinkled lightly across her cheeks showed. Her long golden blond hair was pulled back tightly into a thick braid, which hung down to her shoulder blades. She looked healthy, vibrant and even younger than her twenty-five years.

"If we're through, I'd better go. Denise will be waiting for me."

"Yeah, we're through. I was just taking a breather before I go back down the hall. I have to tackle Mick about giving me an extra five minutes tomorrow."

"You mean take time away from the news? Good luck!" Maressa, like everyone who worked at the TV station, knew the reputation the news director had for being uncooperative. It would be almost impossible to get him to approve taking time away from one of his precious news programs.

"Thanks. I'll need it." Lynn stubbed out her cigarette in a tin ashtray and rose, gathering up her armload of papers. They walked together out the door of the studio and down the hall toward the lobby. Lynn took the side corridor that led to Mick's office, raising one hand in a silent goodbye to Maressa. Maressa continued along the hall and past the newsroom's glassed-in walls.

As she stretched out her hand to push open the door to the outer lobby, a voice halted her. "Hey, Maressa! Don't you stop to speak anymore?"

Maressa turned to face the six o'clock anchorman, who lounged in the newsroom doorway. "Hi, Doug. I didn't see you." She kept her voice smooth and impersonal.

"Well, I saw you. You're hard to miss. No wonder your show gets the ratings."

Maressa bristled. "Maybe it's because my show's interesting and well done."

Doug Fairman grinned. He was of medium height, with the muscled physique of a man who worked out with weights. His hair was thick and dark, his skin tan and his eyes a bright blue. He was a good-looking man, and he was very aware of it. After his divorce six months ago, he had pursued Maressa, and his inflated ego was such that he couldn't believe she would really turn him down. Maressa had nothing against the man. But neither did she have any interest in him. Though he was two years older than she was, she found him callow and immature and after five minutes of conversation with him, she was bored stiff. Although other women found him attractive, Maressa had never been one to follow the crowd, and she had consistently refused his offers of a date. Finally, when her reluctance failed to deter him, Maressa had taken to avoiding him altogether. She had suspected he was in the newsroom this afternoon; that was why she had walked briskly past it without glancing in the window.

Doug responded with his boyishly engaging grin, moving forward, his hands reaching out to grasp her arms.

Maressa neatly eluded him, sidestepping to the door and backing it open. "Sorry. Can't stop to talk. I'm in a terrible hurry. So long." She gave him a cheery smile and a wave and scampered through the door. Maressa didn't glance back to see his expression, just hurried past the receptionist's desk and through the lobby.

She swept out the front door and stopped to fumble in her purse for her sunglasses. The blazing Tucson sun was murderous without them. She put on the glasses and walked at a less hurried pace to her car. The parking lot was utterly devoid of shade, and Maressa knew her little two-door foreign compact would be like an oven. So she opened the front door and stood waiting outside for a minute while the heat poured out. Leaning back against the car, she studied the squat beige brick sprawl of the television station.

It had been five years since she first came here to
be interviewed for a five-minute spot on "Tucson at
Noon," Lynn's fifteen minutes of local tidbits and
canned national items that followed the noon news.
She had been only twenty at the time and thoroughly scared by the thought of being on television.
Lynn had wanted to do a piece on her because at the
age of nineteen, while she was attending the University of Arizona, Maressa had started her own bakery.

It hadn't seemed odd to Maressa, coming as she
did from a family that specialized in the unusual. In
fact her family regarded her occupation as rather
mundane, the others being engaged in more artistic
pursuits. Since Maressa's mother had always been
more concerned with the happenings in her novels
than with the food her family ate, Maressa had taken
it upon herself at an early age to cook most of the
meals. She had enjoyed cooking, particularly desserts, and as she grew older and tried out more and
more intriguing recipes, her family couldn't eat
everything she turned out. She began giving desserts
away to her mother's friends, and by the time she
was sixteen she had drifted into selling her confec-
tions to an ever-widening circle of women.

On Lynn's noonday show, Maressa had described
with her easygoing charm how her business had
mushroomed until she had decided to lease a subur-
ban storefront and start a full-time bakery. In the
year it had been in operation, the bakery had turned
a profit. After the TV show, its business increased.
Lynn, spurred by the many letters praising Maressa's segment on the show, had invited her back

six months later. Less scared this time and encouraged by the effect the first show had had on business, Maressa had returned. After chatting a little with Lynn, she had demonstrated a quick, simple dessert.

On the way home, she had come up with the idea of turning the little cooking lesson into a regular thing on the station. The next week she approached Lynn about it. Because of the mail and phone calls they had again received praising Maressa, Lynn was interested.

At first Maressa had taped a five-minute spot once a week, and it was aired on "Tucson at Noon" every Wednesday. Her vibrant looks and personality came through beautifully on the small screen, and she soon built up a following. Before many months passed, the spot was increased to fifteen minutes each week and given its own slot late in the afternoon.

Maressa demonstrated more elaborate recipes and began to add tidbits of information about food and cooking that she found in newspapers and magazines. When she presented the idea of interviewing a local cook each week, the station agreed, a little reluctantly, to expand her show to thirty minutes and add an interview. Maressa's updated show was so well received that the station continued it, though originally the arrangement had been temporary.

Over the past few years, the popularity of the show had increased until now it was syndicated over much of the Southwest, and took up the majority of Maressa's time. With every passing week, she had more and more difficulty coming up with a good interview, interesting tidbits and a recipe that lent itself to demonstration on television. Moreover, Maressa was constantly being asked to give lectures to various groups throughout the state. Last year, she had struck a deal with a publishing company to write a cookbook aimed at the person who worked during the day and wanted a quick, simple and delicious dinner to fix when he or she came home.

As a result, Maressa had too much to do and decided to give up her bakery. It pained her to sell the business she had owned for six years, but it was an established success and she knew that before long she would grow bored with it. The television show and the cookbook, on the other hand, still offered plenty of new opportunities. So, after several months of offers and negotiations, she had signed the bakery over to the new owners only two weeks ago.

She had thought the sale would leave a hole in her life, when in fact she had felt mostly relief. With the extra work of Ken and Denise's wedding, she found her days were completely filled. Overseeing the bakery operations would have exhausted her.

Thinking of the wedding, she decided to stop dreaming about her years with the station, and be on her way. Denise was no doubt waiting for her; she was invariably more prompt than Maressa.

Maressa hopped into the car, wincing at the scorching heat of the vinyl seats. She turned the air conditioner up full blast and wheeled out of the parking lot. The station lay outside Tucson, more than twenty minutes from the bakery. It took the tiny air conditioner that long to finally dissipate all the hot air. The knot at the back of her halter was damp with sweat by the time Maressa reached the bakery and parked.

As she had expected, Denise was waiting for her inside the small, sweet-smelling shop. Although Denise was usually the most patient of people, this afternoon she was pacing the narrow linoleum floor from one display case to another, her hands in almost constant movement, clasping and unclasping, fingers snapping or popping. She jumped at the tiny tinkle of the bell over the door when Maressa entered the store. "Maressa! There you are. I was afraid I'd got the time wrong."

"Nope. I was delayed at the station, that's all." Maressa checked her watch. "Only ten minutes late. That's pretty good for me," she teased.

The thin, dark-haired young woman smiled faintly at her remark. "I'm sorry. You really aren't very late. I'm just nervous today."

"All brides have a right to be nervous this close to the wedding," Maressa reassured her. Denise was such a sweet girl and always so anxious to please; she would be very embarrassed if she thought she had offended Maressa. Since the whole Gaither family was notoriously thick-skinned, it would have been a difficult thing to do, but Denise didn't seem to realize that.

Maressa smiled and took her future sister-in-law by the arm. She walked with her through the swinging half door beside the counter, waving to the woman behind the counter. "Hi, Evie, how's business?"

The blond woman shrugged expressively. "Can't complain. What are you doing back here? Couldn't stay away, huh?"

"Sure. I wanted to see your smiling face." Evie was renowned for her sour visage. "The Holtzes are very kindly letting me make the wedding cake here."

"Oh, yeah, your brother's getting married, isn't he? The good-looking one."

Maressa grinned. "The only brother I have who's old enough to get married. Ben's only ten. This is Denise Taylor, Ken's fiancée. Denise, this is Evie Waller."

Denise smiled and shyly said hello. Evie responded without much interest, her eyes flickering over the girl. Maressa suspected that Evie discounted Denise as someone she couldn't imagine Ken Scott marrying. Frankly, Maressa couldn't quite picture it, either.

Denise was pretty enough in a quiet way. Her hair was thick and black, worn long and straight in a girlish style. Her face was delicately oval, her features pretty and small. Her eyes were wide and gray, almost solemn, and the thick black eyebrows slashing across above her eyes gave her face interest and distinction. But she wasn't as pretty as many girls Ken had met in the past. And her quiet, reserved personality was nothing like Ken's. He was tall, blond and bursting with energy—vivacious and always on the go. People gathered around him, both women and men, whereas Denise was introverted and seemed to avoid people.

The only explanation Maressa could think of for their falling in love was the old cliché, "opposites attract." Perhaps Ken found her restful; perhaps Denise saw in him the excitement and flash that was missing in her own life. Maybe their weaknesses and strengths meshed to make a stronger bond. Whatever the explanation, Ken had fallen for her like a ton of bricks.

Maressa guided Denise into the tiny office in the corner behind the counter. As always, the office was hot, a result of its proximity to the oven area of the kitchen. She motioned toward a chair. "Have a seat. Let me show you some designs from the file."

Maressa pulled open one drawer of the file cabinet and rummaged through it. Beside her, Denise fidgeted on the straight wooden chair. After a few minutes she jumped up and went to examine her face in the tiny mirror on the far wall. She removed a large tortoiseshell barrette from her nape and let her hair fall forward over her shoulders. Combing through her hair with her fingers, she studied herself for a moment, then came back to the chair.

Maressa found the drawings she was looking for and laid them on the desk before Denise. "Here are four cakes I've done in the past that will feed this number of people. Which do you like?"

Denise glanced at them briefly. "This one. No... oh, I'm not sure. Which one do you like?"

"Well, they're all attractive," Maressa hedged. She had discovered that it was difficult to get Denise to make up her mind. All too often Maressa was afraid that she and her sister were the ones who wound up making the decisions for Denise's wedding, which really wasn't right. Denise might feel in the future that her wedding had hardly been hers but really the Scott family's. "I think the one that appeals most to you would be the proper one to have."

Denise frowned, glancing at them again. "I...oh, this one, I suppose. Whatever you think's best. I'm sure you'll make the right decision. They're all lovely. You're far better at this sort of thing than I am." Denise ambled away, returning to the mirror. She squinted at her image and replaced the barrette she had taken out only moments before. "Maressa, what do you think? Does my hair look better with or without this thing?"

"You're very attractive either way," Maressa assured her. She didn't know Denise well, but the way she was acting this afternoon seemed distinctly odd.

Though Denise had trouble making decisions and often waffled for hours, she had heretofore been entranced with every detail of the wedding. In fact Maressa would have said she was a starry-eyed romantic who was living out her childhood fantasy. Yet today she appeared uninterested in the design of the cake. She was also nervous and unusually preoccupied with her hairstyle.

"Denise, is something bothering you?"

The girl whirled. "How did you know? I mean, why should something be bothering me?"

"I don't know. Maybe it's just prewedding jitters. But you keep twitching and jumping up to look at yourself in that mirror, which is hardly big enough to show one eye, anyway. And you aren't interested in the wedding cake."

Denise sighed and chewed at her full bottom lip, the only sensual feature in her dainty, fairy-princess face. "My father's flying into the airport soon. In fact, I'd better leave in a few minutes to pick him up and bring him out to the house." Her face brightened. "Say, Maressa, would you come with me?"

Maressa's jaw dropped. "But surely you don't want me tagging along when you see your father! You'll want to talk to him alone, catch up on each other's news. I'd be in the way."

"Oh, no, truly you wouldn't!"

"It's not that I wouldn't like to meet him, but since he'll be staying at our house until the wedding, we'll have plenty of time to get acquainted."

"I'd really like you to come."

"But what will he think of me, showing up like this?" Maressa looked down expressively at her well-worn jeans, halter top and flat sandals. "I'm hardly dressed to meet anyone."

"He won't mind," Denise assured her eagerly. "I promise. He won't even notice. He never pays any attention to what I wear. Please? You see, I...I'm kind of uncomfortable around him. My father and I have a lot of trouble talking."

Maressa frowned, puzzled. She couldn't imagine feeling awkward around her own easygoing stepfather. However, she had learned long ago that her family was unique. Probably most nineteen-year-old girls found it hard to talk to their fathers. "Well, okay," she agreed. "I don't have anything to do for the rest of the afternoon, anyway. And if it will make you less nervous..."

"Oh, yes, yes."

"All right. Well, which cake shall we choose?"

Denise sat down to study the drawings more carefully this time. Finally she said, "I think this one might be a little prettier."

"Okay, that's it, then." Maressa whisked away the file and drawings, marking the one Denise preferred, and put them back in the file drawer. "Shall we go to the airport?"

Denise nodded and Maressa picked up her purse, leading the way back out of the shop. She headed for her car, unconsciously assuming command, as she always did with Denise. Although there was only a six-year age difference, she felt as if she were an adult and Denise was almost a child. Maressa wasn't sure whether she herself was old beyond her years or Denise was immature for her age. Perhaps it was a little of both.

Maressa paused in the middle of unlocking the door to her little red Datsun. "But wait—what about your car?"

"Oh." Denise glanced toward the silver Honda sports car in question. "I, uh, why don't we just drive by the dorm, and I'll leave it there? Then Ken can bring me back this evening."

"Okay. I'll follow you."

Denise hurried back to her car and jumped in. She started it and was off with a speed that surprised Maressa. Following her, Maressa decided that Denise must take out all her aggression at the wheel. She was hard put to keep up with her as she dodged in and out between cars and screeched around corners. Maressa was grateful when Denise stopped in front of the palm-shaded dormitory where she lived.

When Denise joined her a little breathlessly, Maressa put the car in gear and started for the airport at a more conservative pace. For a while they were silent, then Maressa asked idly, "What's your father like?"

Denise cast her a puzzled glance. "What's he like? I don't know. Like a father, I guess. I haven't really been around him much. He sent me off to boarding school when I was fourteen. And before that, well, he brought me lots of presents and stuff, but he was never at home much. When I was a kid, he started out with this little flying service that my grandfather left him. It wasn't much, but he built it into one of the most successful commuter airlines in the country. He's very forceful and dynamic, you see."

Yes, I do see, Maressa thought grimly. She saw a lonely, timid little girl who had been given an excess of riches but not enough love. She saw a father who was an ambitious man and had no time for his daughter. No wonder Denise was so quiet and retiring, so dependent on others. No doubt she was used to having all her decisions made for her. Maressa was sure Kenyon would oblige her in that respect — although she wasn't sure it would make for a happy marriage for either one of them.

When they had parked at the airport, Denise hurried to a bright green-and-white ticket counter to check the flight information. "Oh, dear, it's on time. We'd better hurry."

"Is that your father's airline?" Maressa asked as she strode comfortably alongside Denise, whose shorter legs were almost trotting.

"Yes. Daddy expanded to a regional company by using lower fares and greater efficiency. Now it's practically nationwide. He's an excellent business-man."

Maressa let out a low whistle. "I *am* impressed."

When they arrived at the proper gate, passengers were already streaming into the waiting room. Denise scanned the area anxiously, her hands clenched on the low railing separating the hallway from the departure lounge. Maressa felt a spurt of resentment toward the father who inspired such anxiety in his daughter. Just then a tall man entered the room and Denise straightened.

"Is that your father?" Denise nodded, and Maressa gave the man a closer inspection. He didn't look old enough to be either a father or a business magnate. His hair was darker than his daughter's, a rich deep black not touched by gray. His impatient stride was that of a young man. He was dressed in a light beige business suit, but his tanned skin and firm, broad-shouldered body suggested an out-doorsman more than an executive who sat behind a desk all day. His jaw was firm, his mouth set in un-compromising lines. Maressa decided Denise must have inherited her delicate looks from her mother.

Taylor spotted Denise, and a smile softened the hard features. He started walking in their direction, and Denise, smiling, skirted the railing to go to him. Maressa trailed uncomfortably behind her, feeling very much a fifth wheel in the situation. Taylor reached out to his daughter and gripped her arms, then pulled her close. Maressa stood apart from them and studied Taylor's face. Up close, she could detect some resemblance to Denise in the man's thick black brows, gray eyes and sensual lower lip. But where Denise's eyes were warm, this man's were piercing and hard, almost silver in color. His mouth was set in a way that indicated he exercised full control over the sensuous side of his nature. He was a man of great appetites, Maressa thought, but he kept them tightly leashed.

Now why had that thought popped into her head? She hardly knew the man. Besides, it was a rather disturbing thing to think about a man who was probably old enough to be her own father!

He and Denise stepped apart. Maressa noted that his hands were clasped behind his back as tightly as Denise's were. "Hello, daddy," Denise said softly and glanced down.

"Hello, sweetheart."

"Did you have a nice flight?"

"Yes, very." There was an awkward pause. "How are you?"

"Oh, great, just great. I feel...terrific." Denise shot Maressa a clearly beseeching look, and Maressa went to her rescue. She stepped forward, and for the first time Taylor's hard gray gaze fell on her. Maressa felt the impact of his eyes clear down to her toes, and suddenly she had the feeling that this wedding was going to turn out to be a lot more interesting than she had expected.

2

DENISE MADE THE INTRODUCTIONS BRIGHTLY, grateful for having something to say. "Daddy, this is Maressa Scott, Ken's sister. Maressa, this is my father, Rynn Taylor."

Maressa felt strangely breathless, but she managed to keep her voice even as she extended one slender, capable hand to him. "Mr. Taylor."

Rynn hesitated slightly, his eyes turning a dark gun-metal gray, then enfolded her hand in his. His palm was dry and warm, slightly roughened by calluses. Maressa's throat tightened. She was suddenly very aware of her careless appearance. She hadn't even taken the time to dab on any lipstick! She must look a fright.

"Hello, Maressa. It's nice to meet you," he greeted her, his baritone voice brisk. "Please call me Rynn. 'Mr. Taylor' seems a trifle formal among future in-laws, don't you think?"

"Rynn," Maressa agreed and reluctantly pulled her hand from his.

They strolled toward the baggage-claim area. Since it was obvious that Denise had no intention of keeping a conversation alive, Maressa took over the job. She never had any trouble talking, she thought with an inward smile. "I'm afraid we were almost late. I never expect flights to be on time. But, then, I suppose this one would be the exception, with the owner of the company on board."

Rynn grinned, and the whole quality of his face changed. He seemed younger, happier. "You haven't kept up with the news. I'm no longer the owner. I sold almost a year ago. Denise, are you that close-mouthed with your future relatives?"

Denise stiffened slightly, and Maressa cut in quickly, "Don't blame her. When you meet my family, you'll realize it's hard for anyone else to get a word in edgewise. Why did you sell?"

"The economy," he explained with a shrug. "I love flying, but I'm a realist. It was obvious that airlines were in for hard times. Besides, I'd gone as far as I could in that field. So I'm starting all over again."

"In what?"

"Something related. At least, it has to do with airplanes. I started an air-courier service. We send express packages and letters from place to place."

"And do you enjoy it?"

"Yes. There's a lot of pressure included, but fortunately I've got good managers who take care of most of the problems. I'm able to spend a good deal of time at my ranch in Florida."

That explained the tan and the calluses, Maressa thought. "Your ranch?"

"Yes. I raise horses and prize cattle, mostly Charolais."

"I see. That must be very satisfying."

He smiled again. "How'd you guess?"

"By the way your eyes lit up when you mentioned it," Maressa retorted playfully.

"Yes, I love it. It's as much a vocation as a hobby, I think. Physical labor's good therapy, and there's nothing like a fast gallop to blow away all the cobwebs that a week in the business world builds up. Do you ride?"

"A little. We have a stable of horses, but that's really my sister Annie's domain. I ride, but she's the one who takes care of the animals." They reached the baggage carousel and stopped. "I'll get the car and bring it around to the front," Maressa offered. "That way you won't have to lug your bags all the way across the parking lot in this heat."

"That's all right. I'll manage. I travel lightly—only one bag."

"It's no bother. Besides, I imagine you aren't used to our heat. In the summer it's often over 110." She lifted a hand in a goodbye gesture and started away. She was surprised to find that Denise trotted after her.

"I'll go with you."

Maressa blinked and started to ask if Denise didn't think she should stay to visit with her father, but she clamped her mouth shut over the words. It wasn't any of her business. Nor was the faintly puzzled, almost despairing expression on Rynn Taylor's face as he stared after them. Maressa was beginning to change her opinion. Rynn didn't ignore his daughter. But he seemed as incapable of father-daughter communication as Denise did, as disappointed and frustrated—and as scared, as well?

As the two women stepped out of the terminal into the blazing Arizona sun, Denise commented in awe, "How did you do that? I've never heard daddy talk so much or so easily to a stranger."

Maressa shrugged. "It's one of my talents. Ken can act; mom writes; Jess thinks up computer programs. I can get people to talk. I think it's what made my business successful. People would stop by the bakery for a cup of coffee and a piece of my pastry. They'd say a few words, I'd respond, and pretty soon they'd be discussing all their problems. Most of my customers were long-time regulars. And, of course, my television show is all talk. The interview is what makes my program. Somehow I can draw out the most reticent people until they chat freely about their successes and failures in cooking. The failures can be highly entertaining, believe me."

They crossed the parking lot in the searing heat and opened the car doors. Even hotter air poured out. "I'll sit in the back," Denise offered. "Daddy's legs are so long, he'll be a lot more comfortable in front."

Maressa suspected that more than politeness had prompted the gesture. Denise wouldn't be expected to enter the conversation if she was sitting in the back seat. It would be left to Maressa to entertain her father. Sighing inwardly, Maressa maneuvered out of the parking space and drove to the front of the terminal. "You know," Denise commented wistfully, "I can't imagine doing what you do. You're only a few years older than me, but you've done so much already! You know how to handle people. I can hardly balance my checkbook, while you've owned and sold a whole business. You're sort of like daddy, only far more pleasant and easier to talk to, of course.''

"Why do you have so much trouble talking to him?'' Maressa couldn't keep herself from asking. That was her trouble: she was always getting herself involved in other people's problems. She couldn't resist asking about them, and then she couldn't resist trying to solve them. Ken told her she was a "helper.'' There were times, however, when she was afraid that she was simply a busybody.

"I have trouble talking to anybody,'' Denise moaned. "But especially him. He's so...oh, I don't know. He's perfect; he always knows how to do things and what to say. And I don't know how to do anything. I'm sure he'll think whatever I say is dumb and useless. He expects me to be able to tell him something and be as concise and unemotional as one of his employees. And, of course, I stumble and mumble around. Besides, he's standoffish. He's never been friendly. You know what I mean?''

"Not really.'' Maressa thought of Rynn's smile. "He seemed nice to me. Maybe a little...'' She groped for the right word to describe Rynn's slight stiffness and the set quality of his features. "Determined and unbending.''

"Unbending!'' Denise repeated firmly. "You hit it right on the head. He's uptight, very rigid. He's always in a hurry. And he's so grim. He hardly ever laughs. I couldn't believe the way he smiled and looked so relaxed with you. It's not at all like him.''

Maressa wondered why a man who had such a beautiful smile would choose to look severe all the time. It seemed a shame; Rynn's smile was charming. No, not charming exactly. More like...seductive. She paused, considering the thought. It was odd that she should think of a man Rynn's age in such terms. But, really, there was no other word for it. The slow curving of his lips had had a definitely unsettling effect on her pulse. He definitely had a sexy grin. And why not? Just because a man was old enough to have a daughter of marrying age didn't mean he was over the hill. He could be as sexy as anyone else. Just how old was he, anyway? And where was Mrs. Taylor? It occurred to Maressa that she had never heard Denise mention her mother. She must be out of the picture somehow. Suddenly Maressa wanted to know all the particulars. It seemed very strange that she had never asked Denise about it before.

She pulled up in front of the baggage-return area, and the two of them went inside. They found Rynn standing by the conveyor belt full of slow-moving baggage, one foot tapping impatiently. At last a large leather suitcase slid onto the belt, and he circled a knot of people to grab it. Maressa again led the way outside into the dazzling sunlight. Rynn stopped and fumbled in his pocket for a pair of aviator sunglasses that were mirrored on the outside. After he'd slipped them on, it was impossible to see his eyes. The dark glasses made him look even more remote, but also very attractive. The rugged, silent stranger,

Maressa thought, then grimaced—it sounded like a Clint Eastwood movie. she unlocked the small trunk of her car, and Rynn set his bag inside, almost filling it. Then he folded his tall frame into the front passenger seat. The corners of Maressa's mouth twitched at the sight of him sitting with his knees almost touching his chin.

"You should have warned me, Denise," she teased. "We could have brought mother's car. I'm sorry there's so little leg room, Rynn."

"That's all right. I've ridden in worse," he lied valiantly.

Maressa put her foot to the accelerator and they chugged off. The air conditioner was barely able to keep the air even lukewarm with the added heat of three bodies in the car, especialy in the slower city traffic. Maressa was intensely aware of Rynn's presence beside her. It wasn't long before he began to struggle out of his suit jacket, something of a feat in the close quarters. Next he loosened his tie and unbuttoned the neck of his shirt. In a few more minutes, he unknotted the tie and removed it altogether. He unfastened another button, then his cuffs, rolling the sleeves up to his elbow. Maressa smothered a smile as she watched him out of the corner of her eye. She wanted to ask how far his strip show would go, but she decided their acquaintance was too brief for that flip remark. After all, Rynn was a father, however little he looked like one, and a stuffy executive to boot. He might not appreciate her humor at his expense. Besides, the thought of stripping in connection with Rynn, even in jest, caused a strange fluttering sensation in her abdomen. Better not to think about it.

"Tell me about your ranch," she said, to get her mind off the topic.

He glanced at her, surprised. "What would you like to know?"

"I don't know. Anything. I don't know much about ranching. And Denise will tell you I'm terminally curious about anything and everything."

"Well, as I said, I raise mostly horses and prize cattle. It's rather a small operation compared to most Western ranches, I imagine. I bought it for tax purposes, but I love to ride and over the years I've spent more and more time there. It's very relaxing. Of course, I have a foreman who's there full-time. I don't really do much in the way of overseeing operations. I just go down there from time to time and look at the stock and pretend I know what the manager's talking about."

Maressa chuckled. "Somehow I doubt that you're quite that ignorant. Where in Florida is your ranch?"

"In the upper central portion, not too far from Atlanta."

They continued to chat for a few more minutes, then fell silent. Maressa was glad, for she had been having trouble keeping her mind on what Rynn said. Her thoughts were far more occupied with the sight of his firm thighs on the bucket seat beside her, the gray cloth sticking to his damp flesh and molding against his muscles. Fine black hairs lay against

his forearms, bared by the rolled sleeves. His skin
glistened with perspiration. His hands rested lightly
on his knees. Maressa had a sudden crazy urge to
reach out and slide her fingers along his arm, to
feel the tickle of the hairs and the slickness of the
sweat, the wide bones and knobby outcropping of
his wrist, then on to the hands, so hard and corded,
yet strangely sensitive, with their long slender fingers. She swallowed, remembering his light touch
when they shook hands, imagining his hand on her
leg, sliding smoothly upward....

Maressa almost missed a turn and yanked the
steering wheel in dismay, sending them screeching
around the corner. Rynn swayed with the sudden
movement of the car and his arm brushed hers, hot
and electric. Why was she having such thoughts?
And why did his slightest touch disturb her so? She
had met lots of men in her television work and not
one, not even the most handsome or suave, had affected her like this. She had never had sensual fantasies about a stranger before—or even about someone
she knew, for that matter! It was crazy. Bizarre. She
didn't know what to make of it.

But if she didn't concentrate more on her driving,
they were going to wind up in an accident. Grimly
Maressa clutched the steering wheel and focused her
attention on the road in front of her.

They were soon out on the desert. The arid
ground stretched around them, dotted sparsely with
cacti, chief among them the tall, armed saguaro.
Blue-tinted Mount Lemmon shimmered in the dis-

tance. After a few minutes, Maressa turned off the highway onto the Gaithers' dirt road, slowing down considerably to accommodate the bumps and ruts.

Rynn's face was set in harsh lines, and Maressa was sure he was beginning to doubt that they would ever get out of the dust and heat. The landscape became uneven, broken by huge boulders and gullies. They rounded one of the gigantic rocks, and before them lay the sparkling white Spanish-style house of Maressa's family. She pulled to a stop in the circular gravel drive in front of the house, and Rynn gratefully unfolded from the car.

The house was shaped like a U, with two wings extending frontward and a courtyard lying between them. A whitewashed wall with a black wrought-iron gate completed the square. Maressa opened the gate and led her guests through the courtyard. A fountain splashed hypnotically in the center of the rock-and-cactus garden. A tiled walkway ran to the covered porch and the double doors, ornately carved in the Spanish manner. Maressa opened the door, and they stepped into a welcome blast of frigid air.

There was a clicking of nails on the bare tile floor, and a large mongrel bounded into the hall. Snuffling madly, he leaped first on Maressa, then on Rynn, greeting the stranger with a notable lack of suspicion. "The only way you'd thwart a burglar is to lick him to death," Maressa scolded, hooking a hand under his collar and hauling him off Rynn. "Benedict! Come get your man-eating dog!"

Seconds later, a small, earnest-looking ten-year-old boy burst into the hallway. "Maressa! Gee, I'm sorry. Here, Willie, here, boy." He snapped his fingers and the dog bounded over to him, wriggling in delight. Benedict examined Rynn gravely, one hand absently scratching his dog's head. "Hi. Who are you?"

"This is Denise's father, Rynn Taylor. Rynn, this is the owner of the hound who just attacked you. My brother, Benedict Gaither."

"How do you do?" Rynn greeted him solemnly and extended his hand. The boy grinned and gave it a firm pump.

"Hi. Do you like baseball?"

Rynn blinked, seemingly taken aback by Benedict's blunt, direct manner, but he answered promptly and with enthusiasm, "Sure. Sometimes, when I'm in Florida, I go to spring training."

"Really? Gee, I'd like to do that."

"Perhaps sometime you could visit me, and we could go together."

"Really? That'd be great. Do you think I could, Maressa?"

"I don't know. We'll see. First you'll have to wait until Mr. Taylor invites you. Then it will depend on a few other things, like school."

Benedict's grimace dismissed such mundane matters, and he launched into an animated description of the last Dodgers game he'd seen on television. Finally Maressa covered his mouth with one hand. "Enough. You'll drive Rynn away before he's even settled in. Scoot. I'm going to show Rynn to his room and give him a chance to rest."

"All right," Benedict agreed reluctantly and walked away, pulling Willie after him.

Maressa led Rynn and Denise through the great rambling house, pointing out the patio in back and the swimming pool beyond it. Finally they reached Rynn's room, and Maressa opened the door to show him the large bedroom carpeted in blue and furnished with massive, dark furniture that looked as if it might have come out of a Spanish mission. "You share a connecting bath with Ken," Maressa explained, crossing the room to adjust the blinds against the afternoon light. "I'm afraid you won't be able to meet mom and dad yet. They're holed up in their respective studies and woe betide anyone who disturbs them. I'm going to fix myself a gin and tonic. Care to join me? Oh, I didn't think. You two might rather talk alone for a while."

"Oh, no," Denise put in quickly. "We'll join you in the den in just a minute."

Maressa thought she saw a flash of disappointment cross Rynn's face, but it was gone as quickly as it came. He added, "Yes, of course. That sounds like just the thing to pick me up after the trip."

Maressa smiled and walked away, going down the long hallway to the den. There was definitely a lack of closeness between Rynn and his daughter. She wondered why. Rynn was a little stiff and silent, but she sensed warmth beneath the stern exterior. Maressa smiled to herself; perhaps that was just her own wishful thinking.

She strode to the bar in one corner of the red-tiled den and took out three glasses. After pouring in gin and tonic, she squeezed half a lime into each drink and added ice cubes. The clear, fizzing drink was cool and citrusy and lowered one's temperature simply to look at it. Maressa carried the glasses over to the game table on the other side of the den, beside a plate-glass window that looked out onto the patio and swimming pool. Flowers bloomed in bright profusion under the protection of the house's overhang. Elizabeth Scott had moved to Tucson seventeen years ago as a young widow, and she missed very little about the East except the beautiful flowers she had known in Virginia. So she did her best to keep at least a border of flowers around her patio, watering them lovingly every day.

Maressa took a sip of her drink and sighed in contentment. It was a heavenly antidote to the heat, so cold it almost closed her throat. As she rested, gazing idly at the sparkling blue surface of the pool, she heard loud voices in the bedroom wing. Who could it be? The deep male voice didn't belong to either Jessie or Ben, and her stepfather and mother never quarreled. Usually any raised voice belonged to Ken or herself. Then a door slammed, and moments later Denise stalked into the room. She plopped down on a high stool in front of the bar, her face set in a mulish look of anger. After a moment, she glanced around and spotted Maressa observing her with interest. A sheepish expression crossed her face. "I'm sorry. Could you hear us in here?"

"Not clearly. Just the tone. Were you having a fight with your father or has Ken come home?"

The girl looked shocked. "It was my father. I never fight with Ken!"

Maressa smiled wryly. "Don't worry, you will. I

find Ken to be one of the easiest people to fight with
I know. The artistic temperament, I suppose."

She studied Denise, her head tilted to one side.
Perhaps she didn't know much about true love; certainly she had never been in perfect agreement with
anyone, let alone Ken, who was both opinionated
and variable. She wondered briefly about Ken and
Denise's relationship. Their courtship had been very
short. Maressa wondered if they had had the time to
get to know each other at all. How would Denise
with her retiring nature be able to cope with Ken's
volatile personality?

"What were you and your father fighting about?
That is, if you don't mind my asking?"

"Oh, no, it's nice to have someone to talk to. It's
one of the things I like best about your family. You
talk to one another so much. Daddy and I hardly
ever say a word. We were fighting about the wedding, naturally."

"Is he upset because you preferred to have it
here?"

"I don't think that bothers him. I mean, since mother's dead and we don't have many relatives, it doesn't
make much difference where I get married. Daddy is
more transportable than your whole family."

"We are quite a brood," Maressa admitted, thinking with dismay of the impending arrival of her
various aunts and uncles.

"I love your family," Denise confided. "I enjoy
being here, listening to you talk and seeing you hug
and kiss one another. It makes me feel warm inside,
as if I were part of the family, too."

"You are. There's no 'as if' about it," Maressa assured her sincerely.

"Dad doesn't care where I get married. He doesn't want me to marry at all."

"Does he have something against Ken?" Maressa's sisterly loyalty stirred.

"He hasn't even met him. But he doesn't much like people in general. I guess he thinks they're a waste of time. All dad's interested in is making money. I was surprised when he accepted Elizabeth's invitation to stay here this week. I figured he'd fly in the night before the wedding, stay in a hotel and fly out the next day."

Maressa giggled. "I'm afraid he's in for a shock. If he doesn't like people the Gaithers and Scotts are going to set him back on his heels. Two of my aunts are coming tomorrow, and they make the rest of the family look positively straitlaced. And if Uncle Martin should show up... Well, your father will probably run for his life!"

Her momentary gloom lifted, Denise burst into laughter as Maressa had intended. "Oh, no, dad would be too proud to run. He'll just get stiffer and stiffer." She sighed. "I don't know why he's so solemn and serious all the time. He's such a stick-in-the-mud! That's why he doesn't want me to marry Ken. 'It's not proper.' He doesn't believe in being spontaneous or in laughing and having fun. No doubt his plan was to marry me off to some business associate so it would be profitable to him," she concluded bitterly.

Having seen Rynn with his daughter, Maressa felt

that Denise was wrong about her father's motives. However, she knew better than to argue with a person who was upset, so she kept her mouth firmly shut.

Steps sounded in the hallway and Denise leaped to her feet. "Uh-oh. I'd better go or we'll get into another fight. I think I'll see what Jessie's up to. Bye."

Denise slipped out the sliding glass door just as Rynn stepped into the room. A ghost of a smile touched his lips as he walked over to Maressa, sitting at the table. "It looks like I frightened Miss Muffet away."

"Something like that," she agreed noncommittally. Rynn had changed into casual white trousers perfectly tailored to his trim legs and a blue-and-white striped top. Its short sleeves revealed corded arms, and the wide V-neck opened to expose his tanned throat and the jutting collarbone below. The hollow of his throat was a deep indentation. His very presence flustered her. She made a nervous gesture toward the drinks on the table. "Sit down. I fixed you a gin and tonic. I hope that's all right."

"It's fine." He pulled out a chair and sat down, crossing his legs so that the ankle of one rested on the other knee. He took a long sip of the clear drink and sighed. "Mmm. Perfect." He raked a hand through his hair and gave Maressa a twisted smile. "I'm afraid my daughter and I rarely see eye to eye. Is that the lot of parents, or is it just me?"

"I don't know. I've always gotten along well with Lionel—that's my stepfather—but it would be pretty hard not to. Some of my friends had trouble with their fathers. Why do you and Denise have problems?''

Rynn shrugged. ''We don't communicate well on any subject. It's my fault, I suppose. I've never been a very good father to her, the kind of father she needs. When she was young my business was just getting started, and I spent all my time on it. I wasn't around much. I gave her gifts thinking that would express my love. Now I realize it didn't; what she really needed was my attention. But I was too young and foolish to know it then. Too young to be a father. With a son I could have roughhoused, played sports, but with a daughter...I didn't know what you did with a daughter, except adore her from a safe distance. She seemed so tiny and fragile, I was always afraid I might hurt her.

''After she became a teenager, it was ten times worse. I knew there were things she needed to learn, needed to talk about, but I didn't have the slightest idea how to go about it. She really needed a mother then, but her mother died when Denise was fourteen. After her mother's death, I decided to send Denise to a boarding school. That was when the gulf really opened between us. I thought it would be the best thing for her. She'd always been a lonely child, and I thought that living in a dormitory she'd have the chance to be with other girls her age and make friends. I was away on business a lot, which meant she would have had to spend many of her days and nights with a housekeeper. A boarding school seemed like the perfect solution.''

"I take it Denise didn't think so?"

He grunted. "Hardly. I've been a tyrant ever since, in her eyes. She didn't want to go, but I thought she was just being cowardly, and I forced her to go, anyway. She decided that I wanted her out of the way so I could carry on my business more easily. She believed I loved my business more than her. Having just lost her mother, she felt like she'd lost her father, too. Denise hated the school, didn't make friends with the other girls. But she's so quiet, so introverted, that she didn't tell me. It was almost two years before I found out that she hated it there and was utterly miserable. I brought her home then, of course, but it was too late. The damage had been done. She was convinced I didn't care about her, positive I would never listen to her or give her wishes and ideas any consideration."

A grim smile quirked the corners of his firm mouth. "I messed it up pretty thoroughly, I guess."

Pity twisted Maressa's heart. "Things like that aren't irrevocable, you know."

"Aren't they?"

"No! Absolutely not. It may take time and effort, but human beings and relationships mend. They aren't like broken toys."

"I hope you're right." For a moment he was lost in reverie, then he straightened and looked at her, smiling determinedly and brushing aside his melancholy. "You said Lionel was your stepfather. Is Kenyon your half brother?"

"No. Ken and Annie and I are mother's children by her first husband. Our father died when Annie was a baby. I was six, and I barely remember him. After he died she moved out here, and then she met Lionel. At the time I didn't think anything about it. I just enjoyed having a father like him. But now I realize how kind he was and what a huge burden he took on: a widow with three small children to care for and support. He never complained, though, and he loved us as if he were our own father. But only the two younger kids, Jessie and Ben, are his children."

"He sounds like a fine man."

"He is. The perfect gentleman—that's how I see Lionel Gaither."

Maressa gazed out toward the pool, and Rynn studied her sculptured profile. She was a fresh, natural beauty, he thought, young and glowing with life. He had seen more beautiful and more striking women, but few whose eyes were so green and clear or so bright with interest and humor. Even devoid of makeup, her cheeks were tinged with color. Her skin looked as soft as down, creamy smooth. And her hair—thick and lustrous in its fat braid, a few wisps escaping and lying damply around her face—how he would have liked to touch it! He wanted to run his fingertips slowly across her pale skin and touch the golden flecks that sprinkled her nose and cheeks.

Sternly Rynn pulled his thoughts back from the direction in which they were headed. Good Lord! What was the matter with him? Had he reached his "midlife crisis"? Imagine hungering after a girl his daughter's age—a friend of hers and her future sister-in-law, too! It was ridiculous, embarrassing.

But he wondered what he would have done if he had met her in some other situation, a different setting. Then he might not have remembered that he was much older than she was and supposedly a levelheaded, sober man.

Maressa turned back from her contemplation of the pool and was startled to find Rynn's intense gaze fixed on her. What was he thinking? She searched for something light and amusing to say to ease the sudden tightness in her chest and throat. "You know, you don't look like a father of the bride."

A slow grin curved his lips. Maressa had the feeling he wasn't used to smiling. "Don't I? And how does a father of a bride look?"

"Oh, Spencer Tracy-ish. White hair, lines. You know."

"I married when I was a teenager," he explained, shrugging. "I was Denise's age when she was born."

By Maressa's quick calculations, that made Rynn thirty-eight years old. Not bad, really. In fact, not that much older than she was. The idea was oddly comforting. "That's awfully young for so much responsiblity."

He grimaced. "Try telling Denise that."

There was the loud tap of heels on the tile of the hallway, and both Rynn and Maressa turned toward the doorway. Elizabeth Scott Gaither paused dramatically in the doorway, then swept into the room.

3

MARESSA NOTED WITH AMUSEMENT that her mother was wearing her usual garb—a loose, flowing purple-and-lavender-patterned caftan that hid the extra pounds, which testified to her love of sweets. Her short, curling hair was the same bright color as Maressa's, but its radiance was dimmed by the flash of jewels adorning her throat, ears and wrists. The word most often used to describe Elizabeth was "flamboyant." "There you are, my dear!" she exclaimed, as if she had been frantically searching for her daughter, and strode toward the table, her gauzy robe fluttering out behind her.

"Hello, mom."

"This must be dear Denise's father. How do you do? I'm Elizabeth Gaither, Kenyon's mother."

Rynn rose politely and shook her hand. "I'm pleased to meet you."

Elizabeth turned away in a swirl of lavender and purple and sat down in one of the chairs. She reached for the third drink, which Maressa had prepared for Denise, not at all surprised to find that what she wanted was already waiting for her. "Ah, gin and tonic," she breathed after sniffing it. She took an elegant sip. "Just the thing. My daughter makes the most delicious cocktails," she told Rynn proudly.

"Uh, yes, it was very good," he replied vaguely, stunned by Mrs. Gaither's outlandish appearance. She obviously didn't resemble his image of a mother.

"I thought you might be outside soaking up some of our sunshine," Elizabeth rattled on. "Maressa, why didn't you take Mr. Taylor out to the pool?"

"There's a little too much of our sunshine out there right now for my comfort," Maressa retorted. "Besides, Rynn has a ranch in Florida. They have sunshine there, too."

"Do you?" Elizabeth turned toward him. "Have a ranch, I mean, not sunshine. Of course you have sunshine. Really, Maressa, sometimes you can be quite rude to your own mother. But I thought Denise was from Atlanta. Isn't she from Atlanta, dear, or do I have her mixed up with someone else?"

"Our main home is in Atlanta," Taylor assured her in his deep baritone.

"Then have two homes? Imagine that. Wouldn't that be nice, Maressa? Where would you have your second home?"

Maressa smiled. She was used to her mother's mental games. "I'm not sure. Seattle, maybe."

"Seattle! Heavens no, it rains too much. I think maybe somewhere in Italy, although they do have all those dreadful kidnappers."

"I would have thought you'd choose a castle in England," Maressa teased, her eyes dancing.

"Too gloomy. Fog. Rain. Ugh. It's only good for

stories. By the way, dear, Lindsay has gotten herself in the most dreadful fix."

"Again?"

"Oh, yes. You know how it is. Her husband's brother is trying to knock her off. He's failed once already, but this time he locked her in a tower room and set fire to the place."

Rynn stared at Elizabeth in a combination of horror and fascination. Maressa laughed. "Lindsay," she explained to him, "is one of mother's damsels in distress. You probably don't know it, but for the past twenty years, mother has been one of the foremost writers of gothic fiction. Her pen name is Beth Kenyon."

Rynn looked even more surprised. "I remember my wife reading your books, Mrs. Gaither. She thoroughly enjoyed them."

"How nice." Elizabeth bestowed a beatific smile on him, then turned briskly back to the matter at hand. "But, you see, Lindsay is the most difficult heroine I've ever dealt with. She keeps walking right into trouble." Maressa was used to her mother's habit of treating her characters as real people over whom she had no control, but it was apparent from Rynn's wary look that he found it a trifle unusual.

"Why don't you let her husband rescue her?" Maressa suggested.

"Well, that would be the thing to do, of course, but the idiot's gone on a trip to London. He was lured away by a false message, naturally. He thinks he can find the secret of Lindsay's origins."

"Oh, is Lindsay's past shrouded in mystery?"

"Definitely. I haven't figured out exactly who her parents are. Perhaps Lord and Lady Grenham."

"Can't you have him realize she's in danger and return from London in time?"

Elizabeth twisted her mouth thoughtfully. "I could, but he'll have to rescue her again at the end. Too much of that can get boring, don't you think? Besides, that's so old-fashioned and dependent. I'd like her to get out of it herself." She stared out the window at the cactus-dotted landscape beyond the pool, her mind far away.

"Mrs. Gaither," Rynn said into the silence, "I wanted to talk to you about this wedding...."

"What?" Elizabeth turned to look at him as if surprised to find him still there. "Oh. Yes, well, you'd better consult Maressa or Anthea about that. They're the ones in charge of the wedding. Maressa's even making the cake. Aren't you, dear?" She glanced at her watch, then rose. "I've just had the most marvelous idea. I think I can get it out before dinner. Goodbye, my love. Mr. Taylor." She hurried toward the door, her caftan wafting behind her.

Rynn stared after her, bemused. Maressa had to press her lips together to keep from laughing. Rynn Taylor was getting quite an introduction to a family that was anything but serious and proper.

After Elizabeth departed, leaving a rather stunned Rynn behind her, Maressa finished her drink and rose. "If you'll excuse me, I think I'll leave now. I'm sure you'll be glad of an opportunity to rest, anyway."

Rynn rose politely. "Thank you for the drink. I've

enjoyed talking to you." He paused, then asked, "Uh, will I see you at dinner this evening?"

"Oh, yes, I'll be there. I live across the pool in the guest cottage." She pointed to the small building beyond the pool. It was a miniature of the main house. "It's a lot easier than living with the family, but I often eat dinner with them." Maressa saw no reason to reveal that she rarely ate with the family and had made up her mind to do so only minutes ago.

"How nice. Then I'll look forward to seeing you later."

"Thank you. Goodbye." Maressa stepped out the sliding glass door and walked past the pool and along a narrow pebbled walkway to the door of her cottage. It was small inside, just one bedroom, a combination living room and breakfast area, a bath and a tiny kitchen. However, it was adequate for her needs and allowed her to maintain a separateness from her family while still enjoying their conviviality. She had redone it when she'd moved in three years ago and it was now cool, pristine and elegant. The walls were painted a pale celery shade, with coordinating wallpaper in the breakfast nook, kitchen and bathroom. The furniture was light in color and finely crafted, chosen with care over the course of several years. It was a restful place, as different as could be from the large, vivid, ornately furnished main house. It was Maressa's retreat from the delightful, but often irritating, chaos that ruled in her family.

Maressa disrobed almost as soon as she walked in the door. After the excessive heat in the car, she felt grimy and sweaty, and she wanted a bath. She ran water in the pale blue marble tub and took a nice long soak. Then, toweling dry, she dressed in a cool yellow sundress that bared her back and a good deal of her chest, hinting at but not quite revealing the soft tops of her breasts. She unbraided her hair and brushed it out into a shining mass that spilled over her shoulders. Not wanting it to appear that she'd made a special effort, she did not add any makeup except lipstick and mascara. Then she dabbed perfume to her wrists and throat and glanced at her watch. The supper, which the housekeeper had made and left in the microwave before she went home, would be ready to eat in approximately an hour. That meant her family would soon start gathering for their usual cocktail hour before the meal.

Maressa left her house and strolled across the patio to the den, anticipation swelling in her chest. Rynn stood at the far end of the den, hands clasped loosely behind his back, peering at the rows of awards and trophies that adorned the shelves. He turned when he heard the swish of the sliding door opening, and his eyes widened when he saw her. Maressa hoped that betokened admiration. She smiled. "Hello. It's almost time for dinner. We usually gather about five-thirty for drinks. Could I fix you another?"

"Are you the official bartender of the family?"

Maressa chuckled, showing white, even teeth. "Actually, it's usually every man for himself, but since you're a guest, I thought I'd be polite."

"Well, although you're a very lovely bartender, I

think I'll forgo a drink this time. Frankly, I'm still on Eastern time. It's eight-thirty to me, and without any food in my stomach I'm afraid I'd meet my future in-laws in an inebriated state."

"Believe me, with my family, they probably wouldn't even notice. I'm sorry. I didn't think about the time difference. I should have offered you something to eat."

"It's all right."

"Let me see what I can find." Maressa opened the cabinets behind the bar and rummaged until she found a can of peanuts. She opened it and plunked it down onto the bar.

Rynn poured a few nuts into his hand and began to pop them one by one into his mouth. "I saw several awards over there from Thespian groups. They seem to be Kenyon's."

"Yes, he's quite good," Maressa assured him proudly. "Even if he is my brother. He's in rehearsal right now for another play. It's too bad you won't see him perform. But maybe you'd like to go down some evening for a rehearsal. Ken would love it. He's not shy about his accomplishments."

"That would be very nice, I'm sure." Rynn traced a scratch on the bar with his thumbnail, then looked out toward the pool. His expression was that of a man searching for a tactful way to express what he wanted to say. "I was wondering, is acting . . . I mean, is it Kenyon's hobby?"

Maressa stared. Obviously Denise hadn't informed her father of her fiancé's occupation. Why did these things always land in her lap? "Rynn," she began as gently as she could, "Ken's *profession* is acting. That's always been his primary interest in life. He's a drama major and plans to go into legitimate theater."

"I see." She had confirmed what he suspected. Rynn's lids shuttered his eyes momentarily. "Apparently Denise neglected to tell me a few salient facts."

Maressa had no answer for that. She knew Rynn was struggling to maintain his calm in front of Ken's sister. She imagined what he'd really like to do was to burst forth with a few well-chosen expletives. It was an awkward moment. Maressa shifted from one foot to the other, searching for something to say. She was saved by the slamming of the front door. A moment later Ken bounded into the room, handsome and brimming with vitality.

"Hi, Mare. Where's Denise? Oh, hello. You must be Mr. Taylor. I'm Ken Scott."

"How do you do, Ken?" Rynn rose somewhat warily and extended a hand, which Ken pumped enthusiastically.

"It's nice to meet you. Has Maressa been taking care of you?"

"Yes. Your sister has been most charming and patient to spend her day keeping a nervous father occupied."

"Don't worry. She loves it." Ken assured him, wrapping an arm around Maressa's shoulders and hugging her. "How about a Scotch and soda, Mare?"

"Coming up." Maressa pulled out a glass and began to fix his drink while Ken slid onto the stool beside Rynn.

He scooped up a handful of peanuts from the can, commenting, "Classy container."

Maressa laughed. "Listen, he's lucky to get that. Rynn just reminded me that his stomach is on a different time zone than ours. And I forgot to ask if he wanted anything to eat."

Rynn smiled, watching Maressa laugh. Her eyes turned brilliant and glittering when she was amused. Looking at her mouth he had difficulty remembering that the young man beside him was his future son-in-law, who had chosen a singularly uncertain career. Ken was rattling on about the play he was in at the moment, a drama for the local theater, but Rynn hardly listened. His thoughts were on Maressa. She was so lovely, so warm, so full of life and humor. She would bring sunshine to any man's life, even his own rather gray existence.

That was a dangerous way of thinking. Rynn pulled his mind back to what Ken was saying, "I'd better go get Lionel. I swear, I'd faint if anyone in this family was ever on time." He jumped off the bar stool and left the room.

While they waited for Ken to return with his stepfather, a slender blond girl entered the room. She was pretty, though without the flash her brother and sister possessed. "Rynn, this is my younger sister, Anthea. Anthea, this is Denise's father, Rynn Taylor."

The girl tossed back her mane of hair and regarded him seriously from under the fringe of her bangs. "Hello."

Rynn found her gaze disquieting and searched for

something to say. "Uh, Anthea, are you in college, too?"

"Yes, I'm a junior now."

A junior. That would make her about twenty. How old was Maressa then? At least older than he had thought. Dressed now in that almost backless dress and with makeup on and her hair out of the braid, she looked older than she had this afternoon. Was she twenty-one? Maybe even twenty-two? Not that it mattered. She was still far too young for the kind of thoughts he'd been entertaining about her. "What are you majoring in?" He always found it so damn difficult to make conversation with young people—until today when Maressa had had him spouting off about Charolais cattle and ranching.

"Literature. I've changed my major quite often during the past few years, but now I've decided what I want to do with my life."

"Mmm-hmm," Maressa inserted disbelievingly.

Anthea shot her a disdainful look. "Well, I have. I want to write. Not the kind of tripe that mother writes, of course. I'm devoted to serious literature."

"Which means that all her characters will be involved in sex, drugs and contemplating their navels," Maressa explained impishly. "I think you'd be better off to stick with veterinary medicine, Annie, considering how you love animals."

"Oh, Maressa...." Anthea shot her a look of disgust.

Maressa glanced toward the doorway and came around the bar to take Rynn's arm, guiding him toward the two children who had just entered the room. The feel of his smooth, warm skin beneath her hands was electric. To hide her reaction, she introduced her younger siblings with an excess of gaiety, "You remember Benedict, don't you, Rynn? The baseball freak with a dog bigger than he is. And this is Jessamine. She's thirteen and totally devoted to video games."

As Maressa was introducing Benedict and Jessie to Rynn, Ken entered the room with his stepfather in tow. Lionel Gaither was a tall, gentle man with thinning dark hair and a perpetually vague expression. Ken announced proudly, "Rynn, this is our father, Lionel Gaither."

Rynn smiled and shook his hand. "Mr. Gaither, it's a pleasure to meet you. Your children are very fond of you."

Lionel smiled. "Yes, they're very dear. Very dear. I'm glad to meet you. Denise—that is her name, isn't it, Kenyon?—is such a nice girl. Sorry, I'm a loss when it comes to names; I hope you won't be offended. I remember when Ken and Maressa were little, I'd always take them shopping with me, and they would tell me the names of everyone I was supposed to know, so I could greet them without offending anyone. I'm afraid Benedict is no help that way. He doesn't know the names of anyone but baseball players. Confidentially I think he's a bit mad on the subject."

"He seems like a nice boy."

"Oh, of course. Of course. Would you like to see my workroom?"

Rynn looked taken aback by the swift change in

subject, but he responded with a polite affirmative, and followed the other man down the hall into the other wing of the house. Maressa trailed along behind them, aware of her stepfather's habit of neglecting to explain his line of work. Lionel passed Elizabeth's study and opened the next door. He stepped back to let Rynn enter.

Rynn's steps faltered and came to a halt. Inside the room stood a workbench and a drafting table. All the walls were lined with shelves upon which sat toy after toy in various shapes, sizes and states of repair. Rynn swallowed hard, looking as though he'd been tossed into a madhouse. He cleared his throat, groping for a tactful comment, while Lionel stood beside him, beaming proudly.

Maressa quickly explained, "Lionel designs toys for a major manufacturer."

Rynn's face cleared. "Oh, I see." He surveyed the room again with less panic in his eyes.

"Yes, I have several patents. The Johnny Moonjumper was mine, you know." He named a popular toy of a few years before.

"Really? How nice. Well, this is very interesting." Rynn gamely walked to one of the shelves and inspected the toys on it. "I've never seen toys in the process of being built before. I hadn't really thought about how they came into being."

"Of course not. People never do," Lionel sighed, shaking his head sadly. "They don't realize the amount of time and effort that goes into the creation of even a simple toy. Take my Toddle Train." He hauled a wooden model of a train engine off a low shelf. "It's designed for one-year-olds on up. You'd think it would be easy to design, wouldn't you? Well, actually—"

"Lionel, it's time for dinner," Maressa interrupted before he could get really launched on the subject. She knew he could rattle on about toys for hours, perfectly oblivious to time, food or other people.

"Oh." Lionel looked rather crestfallen. Then his expression brightened. "We'll have plenty of time to discuss this later, won't we?"

"Yes, of course." A smile twitched at Rynn's mouth, but he firmly suppressed it. "I'll be here for several days."

Lionel beamed. "Oh, good. It's so nice to meet someone who's interested in toys and games. Many people aren't."

They returned to the den, where Elizabeth and Denise had finally put in an appearance. They trooped into the dining room and sat down at a massive wooden table, chatting, laughing and sometimes scuffling as they went. Supper was the rowdy affair it usually was at the Gaither household, with everyone talking nonstop, jockeying for a place in the conversation. Only Denise and Rynn were quiet. Rynn looked rather shell-shocked.

After dinner, Jessie managed to con Rynn into playing a video game with her. Maressa watched her sister lead him away, and smiled. Poor Rynn had no idea what he had let himself in for. He'd be lucky if he managed to get away in less than two hours. He'd probably be seeing little blips in his dreams that night. Denise and Ken volunteered to do the dishes, and no one fought them for the job. Elizabeth beat a path back to her study, where her conflict was resolving itself on her word processor at a rapid pace. Maressa chatted for a few minutes with Lionel, but then he and Benedict settled down to watch their favorite car-chasing television show and Maressa wandered away. There was a thick novel on the coffee table, and she picked it up and thumbed idly through it. Then, putting it under her arm, she retired to her cottage.

It didn't take her long to discover why the book had been lying around, available. It almost put her to sleep on the couch. Covering a yawn with her hand, Maressa decided to go to bed early. The lights at the main house were still blazing, and as she undressed Maressa wondered idly how Rynn was surviving his first evening in the company of the Scotts and Gaithers. Maressa fell asleep almost as soon as she lay down in her bed, but her sleep was light and disturbed by dreams in which Rynn Taylor seemed to play a leading role.

She awoke late the next morning, still heavy-eyed despite the long night's rest. Yawning, she ran a hand through her tangled hair. What had that last dream been about? It was some crazy thing about a moldering castle in England that could have been the locale for one of her mother's books. Maressa had been locked inside and was beginning to panic, when suddenly the door had burst open and in rushed Rynn Taylor, bare chested, wearing only jeans. He swooped her up from the desk at which she sat and, holding her tightly against his hard chest, had carried her out into the swirling fog.

Maressa shook her head and padded into the bathroom to take a brisk shower and wash away her crazy fantasies. Afterward, as she stood before the mirror blow-drying her hair, clad in a short terry-cloth robe, there was a brisk, authoritative knock on her front door. Maressa turned in surprise. No one in her family knocked; they simply barged in. Brush in hand, her hair a gleaming veil over her shoulders, she opened the door.

Rynn Taylor stood before her, dressed in jeans and a pale blue shirt. Although he was not bare chested, he looked so much as he had in her dream the night before that for a moment she experienced a feeling of déjà-vu. His eyes swept over her, taking in the shining, disheveled mane of blond hair and the brief robe, which revealed a good deal of her shapely legs. Maressa had the impression that Rynn disapproved of her attire for his jaw tightened and he began peremptorily, "Didn't you say your family keeps a stable of horses?"

"Why, yes."

"Good. Perhaps you'd like to come riding with me this morning. I thought I'd start before it got too hot."

"I'd like it very much. Let me slip into some jeans. I'd better warn you, though, to borrow a hat from Ken or Lionel. Even in the morning the sun can easily give you heatstroke."

"All right. I'll meet you at the stables in fifteen minutes."

"Okay. Just take the dirt path beside this house.

The stables are back there among some trees, next to the wellhouse.''

Rynn nodded and strode away, leaving Maressa gazing after him, puzzled and excited. She hurried to her closet and yanked on a pair of new designer jeans. They weren't the sort of thing she usually wore riding, but this morning she preferred to look good rather than sensible. Slipping on socks and boots, she tucked the jeans into the boots and debated the subject of a blouse. Finally she slipped on a rust-colored tube top and a short-sleeved overshirt of rust-and-beige stripes. Pulling her hair up in a bun to keep the back of her neck cool, she secured the loose knot with a few hairpins and donned her wide-brimmed cowboy hat.

When she was satisfied with her appearance, Maressa left the guesthouse and took the narrow path down to the stables. Rynn was waiting for her, holding the reins of two saddled horses and frowning impatiently. When he saw Maressa, the frown disappeared and his eyes moved slowly over her. She wondered if he approved of what he saw. There was nothing in his expression to indicate his opinion.

"Mount up, and I'll adjust your stirrups," he said abruptly, holding out his cupped hands for her to use to vault into the saddle. Maressa was used to adjusting her own stirrups, as well as mounting a horse without assistance, but she accepted the gentlemanly gesture and swung herself into the saddle. The muscles in Rynn's arms bulged as he took her weight, and Maressa's stomach clenched in response. She hooked one leg around the saddle horn while he adjusted a stirrup, then repeated the process with the other leg. Rynn swung onto his horse and they set out at a sedate walk, riding for a long time in silence.

Maressa made one or two attempts at conversation, but they died quickly. Rynn appeared to be brooding about something and finally Maressa gave up the effort, wondering irritably why he had bothered to ask her along when he so obviously didn't want her company. Then Rynn turned toward her abruptly, his expression tight.

His voice wasn't loud, but the tone was nonetheless explosive as he snapped, "Maressa, we have to stop this wedding!"

4

MARESSA STARED agape at Rynn and finally managed to stutter, "Wh-what?"

"I said we have to stop this wedding between my daughter and your brother. I hope you'll help me."

"You must be crazy. The wedding's only three days away."

"I know." Rynn sighed. "I should have done it sooner, but I kept thinking if I left it alone and didn't harangue Denise, she would eventually see reason herself. I didn't want to make her turn stubborn and insist on the wedding just because I opposed it."

"That was wise. Why change your mind now?"

"Because she hasn't called it off!" Rynn barked. He stopped, forcing himself to exhibit a calm he didn't feel.

He had intended to be very reasonable and persuasive, to sell the idea to Maressa the way he would in a business dealing. But the moment he saw her framed in the doorway this morning, dressed in a short robe and looking leggy and luscious, his calm had fled. Now, riding beside her, he found it difficult to keep his mind on the subject. Instead he kept glancing at the puckered top beneath the overblouse, her full breasts shaping the material and the buttons of her nipples clearly evident. He wondered whether she would take off the overblouse because of the heat and let him gaze on her golden shoulders and back. What would she do if he suddenly pulled his horse to a halt, grabbed Maressa and kissed her? Rynn swallowed and tore his mind away. Such thoughts weren't productive or useful. She was a child, like his daughter, beyond his reach. He shouldn't be having such thoughts about her. He must concentrate on the reason for their ride: enlisting her support against the marriage.

"Look," he continued more quietly. "I realize that you're Denise's age and are probably thrilled with the idea of true love. I meant to speak to your parents about it and enlist their aid. I thought they'd see the folly of it, too. But when I met them, I knew that was a lost hope. Frankly, Maressa, you're the only one in your whole family who seems to have any common sense! That's why I decided you were the one I'd have to talk to."

Maressa glared at him. Why had she thought Rynn was a nice man yesterday? And how could she have found him attractive? Denise was right. Rynn Taylor was straitlaced and overly concerned with propriety. She had always been very defensive of her unusual family, and his words raised her hackles. "How dare you make judgments like that about my family! And who gave you the right to decide who should and should not get married? Of all the sanctimonious, overbearing...boors I ever met, you take the prize."

Maressa hauled back on her reins, turning the horse toward the stables, but Rynn reached out and grabbed the bridle. "Hold on a minute. Don't go off half-cocked. I didn't mean any insult to your family. They're very...interesting."

"Oh, please." She rolled her eyes. "Spare me the effusive compliments."

An unexpected grin brightened his face. "I'm sorry. I've made a terrible muddle of the whole thing. As you may have guessed, I'm not the most tactful person around."

"You could say that," Maressa agreed sarcastically.

"I like your father and mother very much. But you have to admit that they're, uh, different from most parents."

Maressa couldn't suppress a chuckle at his cautious description. "All right. I'll accept that."

"They're very nice people," he hastened to add. "But I couldn't envision discussing anything serious with them."

"No," Maressa admitted. "It's not much use. Lionel and mom live in their own little worlds."

"Good. I'm glad you understand why I wanted to talk to you."

"Wait a minute. I see why you chose me instead of mom or Lionel. However, I fail to understand your reason for wanting the talk in the first place. Exactly what is so wrong with this wedding? Is Ken ineligible for some reason? Does he come from too wacko a family or what? And why do you think you have the right to stop it?"

"Because I'm her father!" he roared. His horse skittered nervously and Rynn pulled the reins up short and patted the horse's neck, talking to him soothingly. When he turned back to Maressa, his voice was calmer. "I'm sorry. I keep losing control, but it's only because I'm concerned about Denise. I can't allow her to mess up her life. No, let me finish." He threw up a cautionary hand at the immediate, wrathful glint in Maressa's eyes. "It's not that I have anything against your brother. In fact, I rather liked Ken when I met him last night. But he's wrong for my daughter."

"How can you be so arrogant? It seems to me that Denise is the only one to say who's right and who's wrong for her. She told me you didn't consider the marriage 'proper.' But just because you're a rigid, puritanical, prejudiced person doesn't mean your daughter is!"

"Wait. Who's being judgmental now? I am not rigid, puritanical or prejudiced. At least if I am, those facts have nothing to do with my reasons for not wanting Denise to marry Kenyon. I don't have any objections to the marriage on the grounds of propriety." He sighed. "That's what Denise would like to think because she doesn't want to face the truth. Sometimes she's very good at avoiding reality." He turned to Maressa, his expression almost pleading. "Look, even if Denise and Ken were perfectly suited to each other, they're marrying too young. She's only nineteen! How can she know with whom she wants to spend the rest of her life?"

"How can you be so certain that she's wrong?" Maressa retorted, still seething at the thought that he would object to her brother for any reason.

"Believe me, I know. I've been there myself. I married straight out of high school. I was eighteen years old and so was my wife. We were so much in love that we just couldn't wait." He shook his head, his face drawn in bitter lines. "When Denise was born, I was nineteen—the age Denise is now. That's too young for such responsibility. At an age when I should have been having fun, I was working all day and changing diapers at night."

"She doesn't have to have a baby simply because she gets married," Maressa pointed out reasonably.

"No, but she'd probably do it, anyway. It's as foolish an idea as this one. She's always been a lonely child—"

"And whose fault is that?"

"Mine, of course. I didn't spend enough time with her. I admit I wasn't the best father in the world, but that doesn't make it all right for Denise to make herself miserable trying to banish her loneliness. I think she's fallen in love with your family as much as with Ken. She wants to be a part of that special, loving closeness. What she doesn't see is that she'll be as lonely with Ken as she is now, maybe feel even worse because her great expectations will have been dashed."

"Ken won't be a bad husband!"

He flashed her a sardonic look. "I have my doubts about any twenty-two-year old making a good husband. I'm not saying anything against Ken. He's very nice and I'm sure he'll try. But no one could live up to Denise's ridiculous expectations. She thinks that after she's married she'll never be alone, never be unhappy. She's like a child. I'm afraid that when she finds herself lonely even with Ken, she'll decide that having a baby, someone who will love her totally, would be the perfect answer." He shook his head. "She isn't ready for that. She's too immature. She needs to experience more of life before she can really know what marriage is and what kind of person she should marry."

"Ah, now we're coming to the crux of the matter. Ken isn't the kind of person she should marry, right?"

Rynn ignored the sarcasm. Grooves bit into the skin beside his mouth and eyes, giving him a sad look. "Denise has led a rather sheltered life. Again, it's my fault. Because I felt guilty, because I pitied her for having to live so many years with her mother's illness, I overprotected her. I tried to shield her from many of life's harsh realities. She's shy and, frankly, rather naive. She never had many friends or dated much. I don't think she sees Ken as he really is. She's carried away by his looks and charm. She imagines that he's the person she wants him to be. I think she believes that after they're married he'll change to suit her."

"And how is the real Ken different from her fantasy?" Maressa asked belligerently.

"Look, Ken is very nice and personable. But he's an actor, an extrovert, someone who obviously loves people and enjoys being with them. Denise is none of those things; she's quiet and shy. She prefers spending an evening at home to going out. They'll never get along. When he wants to go to a party, she'll want to stay home. And when she's wanting to snuggle in front of the fireplace in the evening, he'll be out acting in a play or visiting with friends. It's an impossible combination. Besides, Ken has a very forceful personality. I'm afraid he'll sweep poor Denise along in his wake. She won't be able to stand up to him, won't defend herself or argue her side of things. She'll be quietly miserable.''

"Maybe she won't have to stand up to him,'' Maressa began loyally, but then she recalled her own thoughts of the afternoon before. She, too, had wondered whether Denise could escape domination by Ken's forceful, dazzling personality. Nice as Ken was, sometimes he practically had to be hit over the head before he'd pay attention to what the other person was saying. Maressa had worried about Denise's statement that she and Ken never fought. With a person like her brother, that wasn't healthy. Moreover, it wasn't realistic. Was Denise's father right? Did the girl not know what Ken was really like? Did she expect their life to be blissful and smooth?

"You understand what I'm talking about, don't you?'' Rynn saw Maressa's expression and pressed his advantage.

"Maybe Denise has a romantic view of life,'' Maressa admitted. "And Ken is hardheaded and aggressive.'' She grinned, casting Rynn a sideways glance sparkling with humor. "I know because we're so much alike.''

"Some people can handle that,'' Rynn replied gravely and his eyes went disturbingly to her lips, then flickered away. "But not Denise. She's a sweet girl, and she wants a happy, serene life. She's spent too many evenings alone or in sadness." His eyes darkened, and he stared fixedly at the space between his horse's ears.

Maressa frowned, thinking that if Denise's home life had been lonely and sad, probably Rynn's had, too. Impulsively she leaned over and laid a hand on his arm. Rynn's muscles quivered beneath her hand, and he glanced at her in surprise. "I'm sorry," Maressa said softly. "Your life can't have been very happy, either."

Rynn shrugged. "I was an adult. I could take it better than a child. Anyway," he reminded her firmly, "it's Denise we're talking about here, not me."

"My, aren't we prickly?" A smile curved Maressa's lips. Why was it that his abruptness seemed amusing, almost endearing? Was she, like Denise, making up qualities in him that didn't exist, pretending his brusqueness was merely a protective covering for a soft inner self that had been hurt deeply?

With an irritated sigh, Rynn turned toward her. Their eyes locked, hers soft and concerned, glowing with green warmth. Unconsciously Rynn sucked in his breath, and his hand trembled on the reins. He jerked his gaze away. "Come on, Maressa, I'm serious. This is no time for joking."

"You're too serious," Maressa stated briskly. "There's always room for humor. It makes life go down a little easier. Let's say you're right. Nineteen is usually too young to marry. Most girls that age don't know what they want." There were exceptions, of course, like herself. At that age she had known quite well that none of the boys she dated suited her. But evidently Denise had led the opposite kind of life. No doubt her domineering father had taken care of everything for her. "Denise is probably hoping Ken will be like you and run her life for her," Maressa mused aloud. "If so, she's in for a disappointment. Ken's from a background filled with independent women who think and do everything for themselves. His only resemblance to you is probably his stubborn streak."

"I beg your pardon." Rynn sounded faintly affronted, and Maressa wondered if he was teasing her. It was hard to tell from his impassive face. Suddenly he smiled, and the corners of his eyes crinkled up invitingly.

Maressa knew at that instant that there was nothing she would like more than to feel his firm, full lips on hers, and her stomach churned with excitement. This was crazy! Rynn Taylor was a dull, solemn man who'd managed to insult her several times this morning. Moreover, he was thirteen years older than she was and the father of her brother's fiancée. How could she feel attracted to him? "I thought we were supposed to be serious," she snapped.

"It must be catching," he replied, trying to force his mouth back into its usual straight line. Both of them burst out laughing.

"I tell you what," Maressa remarked as her laughter died away. "I think the subject of Ken and Denise's wedding is spoiling a perfectly good ride. I'd enjoy it a lot more if we could just enjoy the sunshine."

"I agree. But it's necessary."

"No. It's not only unnecessary, it's useless." Maressa raised one hand and ticked off her points on her fingers. "Number one, there's not a thing we can do about it. We can't force them not to get married. They're both of marrying age. And somehow I don't think either of us is capable of knocking them over the head and kidnapping them. As you've already discovered with Denise, it would be pointless to try to persuade them it's the wrong thing to do. That's point number two. Number three is that we can't invent some plot to trick them into having an irreconcilable argument. I haven't the heart for it, and I imagine you haven't the acting ability. No matter how much you abhor what Denise is doing, there's no way you can keep her from making her mistakes and suffering the consequences."

"I thought you could speak to your brother, point out the things I've told you about Denise and persuade him that it would be a poor risk to marry her now."

"I'd be the last person who could do that. Ken and I are too much alike. We've fought all our lives. We love each other dearly, but one thing we've learned is not to tell each other what to do. It's disastrous."

Rynn did not reply, and they rode on in silence. The sun was blazing down on them now, and Maressa began to guide her horse back toward the stables. By the time they reached home, the sun would be full strength. She had no desire to stay out in the desert heat, and it wouldn't be safe for an Easterner like Rynn. Maressa glanced surreptitiously at him. He rode slightly ahead of her, his face shadowed by his wide-brimmed hat. A dark line of sweat had dampened his shirt down his backbone and between his shoulder blades. Moisture dotted his neck between his hairline and the collar of the shirt and glistened on his browned arms. His long legs were molded to the horse, thighs gripping firmly, effortlessly. He was very male, Maressa thought... and very sexy. Why did he have to be Denise's father?

Rynn turned toward her. His voice was laced with the pain of a helpless parent. "I can't stand by and watch Denise do something foolhardy!"

"You not only can, I imagine you will have to. There's nothing to be done. If a person wants to act like an idiot, she will. How can you persuade Denise that her marriage will be one way, when she's already convinced herself that it will be something entirely different? Maybe she is fooling herself, but you can't open her eyes for her."

"Then why don't you talk to her? You could explain about Ken and convince her that the marriage won't work."

"It wouldn't do any good. Besides, I balk at criticizing my brother to the girl he wants to marry. There's such a thing as family loyalty, you know."

"Even if he'll be unhappy?"

"What I'm trying to point out is that you have to let people make their own mistakes. That's one piece of wisdom my family knows. It's hard to watch a child do something you're sure will be painful, but there's no other way. Denise is grown up now. Let her live her own life. If you continue to coddle and protect her, she'll continue to be naive, inexperienced and foolish."

"Then you refuse to help me?"

"Right. Not only that, I'd like to convince you not to try to do it yourself. It will only hurt your relationship with your daughter."

Rynn glanced around at the limitless vista. The blue-gray mesas shimmered in the distance. In the early morning and late evening, the sun's rays would turn them blood red or bright golden. A lizard ran across their path and disappeared behind a large boulder. Rynn followed the lizard's path with his eyes, taking in the sprawling prickly pear bursting with yellow flowers and the red-blooming hedgehog cactus. "All right," he sighed. "No more arguing. The view is too pretty. We should see some of it, at least. I promise that I'll think about what you said—if you'll give my words the same consideration."

"That's a deal."

"Good. Now tell me about some of this vegetation. What's that?" He pointed to a cluster of straight green shoots with knobby skin.

"Totem-pole cactus." They continued to the house in pleasant conversation.

After their ride, Maressa retreated to her cottage. She had signed a contract with a publishing company to write a cookbook, and she needed to do some work on it. Besides, she wanted to give Rynn time by himself to think. She fixed a sandwich for lunch and ate in solitude, then returned to work. By four o'clock, she was tired but pleased with her efforts. Leaving her papers piled on the small desk in the bedroom, she rose and stretched, glancing at her watch. There was plenty of time before dinner for a swim. It seemed a fitting reward for all the work she had made herself do when her wayward mind wanted only to think about Rynn Taylor.

Maressa stripped off her clothes and pulled a swimsuit from her dresser. It was a plain turquoise maillot with a splash of flowers along one side. She studied it for a moment, then shoved it back into the drawer and took out a white bikini instead. Slender gold chains fastened the bikini panties on either side. The motif was repeated in tiny chains sewn onto the cloth between her breasts, linking the two cups of the bra. Maressa did not usually buy excessively bare swimsuits, and true to form, this one covered her breasts almost completely while the panties amply clothed her small, firm derriere. It was modest, as bikinis go, but the strips of white material were infinitely alluring against her skin, boldly hinting at the riches beneath the cloth. The little chains added a subtle touch of decadence. Maressa had bought the suit on a whim a couple of months ago, but then had been embarrassed to wear it.

She didn't stop to analyze her reasons for wearing the suit now, but quickly donned it. She wrapped her long hair into a tight knot atop her head and pinned it in place. Grabbing a bottle of suntan lotion and a towel, she headed for the pool. The turquoise water sparkled in the sun, diamonds of light dancing on its surface. Maressa dumped her paraphernalia onto the wrought-iron table beneath the beach umbrella, purposely refraining from glancing at the house to see whether anyone was watching her from the den windows. She dived cleanly into the water and swam several laps before pulling up to the side of the pool to rest, her arms crossed on the rim. Suspended, she lazily stirred her feet through the cool water and eyed the house. The falling sun hit the windows and bounced off, making it impossible to see inside. She wondered if Rynn was there. Just then the door at the end of the bedroom wing opened, and he strode easily across the patio. Maressa sucked in her lower lip to keep from breaking into a smile.

Rynn was even more handsome out of clothes than in, Maressa decided. His shoulders were broad, and the wide expanse of his brawny chest was covered by the same dark hair that adorned his arms. His chest tapered to a narrow waist and hips, the hair disappearing in a V into tight blue swimming trunks. Rynn's legs were long and muscled, though not heavy—the legs of a runner. Maressa felt a warmth stirring in her abdomen. She began to move her legs in a slow scissor kick, unconsciously enjoying the rush of water against her inner thighs.

"Hello." Rynn smiled as he squatted above her at the edge of the pool. "Looks like we had the same idea."

"Yeah. I like a swim before dinner. The pool's nice late in the afternoon."

Rynn sat down and dangled his legs in the water. Maressa was very aware of their proximity to her, and she pulled her eyes away from the line of his thighs. She glanced up at his face, figuring it was a safer target, but her breath caught in her throat at the sight of his eyes. He was watching her, his eyes dark gray, and for a moment a wild hunger burned in their depths. Maressa swallowed nervously. Rynn abruptly turned his head aside and slid into the water, swimming away from her with powerful strokes. She watched for a moment, then placed one foot against the side of the pool and arched onto her back, slowly slicing through the water with a graceful backstroke. She floated and swam lazily for a time, all the while observing her companion out of the corner of her eye. She hoped Ben and Jessie wouldn't decide to join them.

Rynn swam fast, competent laps. Seemingly both his muscles and lungs were inexhaustible. He skimmed along in a straight line, making it easy for Maressa to keep from crossing his path. She moved lazily up and down her own side of the pool, feeling a strange mixture of contentment and frustration. The sensation of water caressing her body was deliciously erotic—like the light touch of a man's hand. Rynn's hand.

She glanced back at him, watching as he curled his legs under him and turned to begin another of his ceaseless laps. She observed the powerful slash of his arms, rising high in the air, then whipping down into the water to thrust back and up. Droplets of water sprayed from his fingertips at each stroke and slid down his arm and back into the pool. The body of water they shared connected the two of them, Maressa thought. It embraced him just as it did her, creating a sensuous bond. She wondered if he felt it, too. Was he shy? Or indifferent?

Maressa grinned impishly. Drawing a full breath, she dived beneath the surface and swam in a path to cross Rynn's. His brown body came into view above her and she pushed off from the bottom, reaching out to grab his foot. He made a surprised noise, then twisted, his long fingers groping for her. For an instant, Maressa feared that she had truly made him angry. Then she saw his face, a white grin belying the sternness of his countenance.

"You devil," he exclaimed, and his hands bit into her waist. He flung her up and back and she splashed loudly, laughing and shrieking, her arms and legs thrashing. He dived after her, and they played like children, chasing and dunking, giggling and gasping for air.

But it wasn't just a game and they both knew that. Slickly their skin slid across each other's with a barely hidden sensuality. Accidentally Maressa's hand touched Rynn's hip, and once he grabbed her from behind and his arm brushed her breast. Her nipples turned diamond hard and pointy at the contact, thrusting plainly against the wet cloth. He saw her response, and it jerked a far more obvious answering cord in his loins. Rynn knew he was playing with fire, but it was such wicked, delightful torment that he couldn't bear to stop. He wondered if Maressa, too, felt the sexual undertones. Was she a tease trying out her powers on an older man?

Rynn broke away, knowing he couldn't continue this way much longer without taking her in his arms and kissing her. As it was, he was aching with desire, wanting to take her in his arms and mold her body to his. He thought of her tongue in his mouth, her lips dotted with drops of water from the pool, cold and tasting faintly of chlorine. He wanted to free her wet hair from its prim knot, to curl the strands around his arm and pull her head to him, holding her captive with his deep kiss.

The sun shimmered on the water, dazzling his eyes. Rynn felt almost dizzy, and he didn't know if it was from the glare or the passion surging hopelessly in him. He swam to the deep end of the pool, his strong arms making it easy to quickly outdistance Maressa. *Old fool,* he told himself as he heaved out of the water.

"Coward!" Maressa called after him teasingly, continuing the pretence of play, but the ache of frustration between her legs was anything but playful. Her nipples were engorged and sensitive to even the slight rub of the wet suit upon them. Her skin was as aroused and tingling as it had ever been after the heavy kisses and caresses of other men. She wondered what Rynn was feeling. Anything? Or had it been just lighthearted fun to him? Why had he suddenly stopped? Was he not interested in her? Or was he too interested? Smiling, she swam to the side and climbed up the ladder. She hesitated for a moment at the edge of the pool, then strolled to one of the yellow-cushioned lounge chairs, picking up her towel on the way and dabbing it against her skin.

Rynn was on a chaise just beyong the one Maressa chose. He lay on his stomach with his head turned away from her. Maressa tossed down her towel and picked up the bottle of suntan lotion. It was a little late for sunbathing, but the sun was blazing brightly, even if it was low in the sky. Standing sideways to Rynn, Maressa squeezed lotion in her hand and languidly began to apply it. Slowly she stroked down one arm, then the other, and came back to do her face and neck.

Out of the corner of her eye, she saw that Rynn had turned his head toward her. Even though he'd put on dark glasses, she knew his cloudy gray eyes were watching her every movement. The thought sent a shiver down her spine, but she merely continued to anoint her body with the lotion, rubbing it on her chest above the line of her bikini. She moved downward over her stomach and abdomen. She sat down, casting a surreptitious glance at Rynn. His hands lay at his sides, clenched into fists that were at odds with the picture of a relaxed sun worshiper.

Swinging her legs up onto the lounge chair, she smoothed lotion onto both of them, then lay back. Her heart thudded in her chest. In truth, the motions meant to excite Rynn had affected her, as well. She had felt his gaze hot upon her, tangible as his touch. And as she had massaged her skin, she had felt as if her hands were his proxy, as if he had been touching her with every stroke.

Maressa wondered why she was carrying on like this. She couldn't remember ever before having acted in such a teasingly sexual manner. She was like a child prodding a dog with a stick. Why? Could she really want Rynn to take her in his arms, kiss her and fondle her? Why, he was Denise's father! He was several years older than she was. He was stiff and uptight and...and unbelievably sexy.

"Maressa!" Annie's voice sailed across the patio and Maressa jumped. "It's almost time for supper. And Aunt Lucille's arrived!"

Maressa sat up reluctantly. Their intimacy was shattered now. "Excuse me," she murmured to Rynn. "I'd better get dressed."

She did not look back as she walked down the sidewalk to her quarters, so she was unaware that Rynn lifted his head and followed her with his eyes, not rising himself until after she had shut her door behind her.

5

Maressa dressed for dinner in a white cotton sundress that was simple, yet feminine and alluring. The straight neckline was supported by narrow straps over her shoulders. The plain bodice buttoned down the front to a fitted waist where the dress then flowed out into a full skirt that reached halfway down her calves. Maressa's small waist was accented by a wide red leather belt, and a touch of sensuality was provided by an eight-inch strip of open latticework across the front of the dress, beginning just above the knees. It revealed only a glimpse of her legs, far less than would have been seen in a dress of normal length, but the openness gave the illusion of daring, of almost risqué exposure. Maressa slid a shiny red bracelet around her arm and put on matching earrings, then stepped into simple sandals with straps resembling thin ropes. Pulling her hair back loosely she caught it in a large barrette at her nape. She applied light makeup, lipstick and mascara. A dab of perfume completed her toilette, and she walked over to the main house.

"Maressa!" Aunt Lucille's voice was trained for the stage and carried easily across the large den filled with talking people. Lucille marched on Maressa with outstretched arms. She was still a beautiful woman, although like her sister she had gradually thickened around the middle throughout the years. Her hair was artfully dyed to its original color, and her face was made up with the finest cosmetics. In tasteful, expensive clothes, she was a mature beauty. Chorus-girl tall, she had to bend to kiss her niece on the cheek and envelop her in a Chanel-scented embrace. "My dear, you look lovely. Isn't a wedding exciting?" She tucked Maressa's hand through her arm and continued in a confidential tone, "The girl's father is an absolute hunk, isn't he? I tell you, if I didn't have my Ham, I'd go after him in a minute."

Her eyes traveled to the couch beside which Rynn stood talking to Lucille's husband, Hamilton Ward. Maressa's gaze followed her aunt's. Rynn did indeed look handsome in a white shirt, white trousers and a dark blue blazer. He glanced up and, seeing her, he smiled. Maressa's knees turned wobbly.

Lucille dragged Maressa toward the couch where Elizabeth and Annie sat beside Denise, while Hamilton and Rynn stood before them. The group was chatting desultorily, and they stopped when Lucille and Maressa approached. "Maressa, my dear girl." Hamilton stepped forward to kiss Maressa on the cheek. Involuntarily Maressa's eyes strayed to Rynn; he was watching her with an expression she couldn't define.

"You know, Lucy," Hamilton said to his wife, "I do believe that Maressa looks rather like you did when you were young."

Lucille bridled a little at her husband's implication regarding her present age, but she stepped back to study Maressa. "Well, her hair is the same color," she admitted reluctantly.

Maressa smothered a smile. Aunt Lucille wouldn't like to be compared to anyone. However, Maressa, too, found it hard to see the resemblance. "Oh, no, I'm not nearly as tall and leggy as Aunt Lucille."

"That's true," her mother agreed judiciously, eyeing her sister and daughter. "But, you know, I can see what Hamilton means."

"It's her figure," Lionel stated calmly, coming up behind them. "Lucy always had an excellent figure."

Lucille smiled widely at the compliment, but Maressa was embarrassed by the searching gazes turned on her. Even though she was accustomed to their frankness, their almost impersonal appraisal made her blush. It seemed different with Rynn Taylor standing there, as if he, too, had been given an invitation to study Maressa's body. She glanced over at him and saw that he was gazing at her, a faint smile lingering on his lips. She looked away hurriedly, so drawn by the relaxed sensuality of his mouth that she was afraid she might throw herself at him in front of everyone.

Soon the whole family was drawn into the discussion of whether Maressa resembled Lucille. Finally Jessie suggested with her usual practicality, "Why don't we get out the old photographs and see?"

"Of course. Go fetch them, Benedict," Elizabeth ordered, and the boy scurried off. He returned moments later and plopped a heavy maroon, leather-bound album down in Elizabeth's lap.

Elizabeth searched for her glasses and finally discovered them on top of her head. She opened the album and bent over the pages of pictures. "Oh, here's a good one," she declared at last. "You know, I think Hamilton's right. What do you say, Anthea?"

She slid the book to her daughter, who studied it with the same care. "They do look alike," she agreed.

Rynn came around the couch and leaned over Annie's shoulder to examine the black-and-white publicity photo of Lucille in her heyday as a Las Vegas showgirl. She was dressed in a skimpy costume that revealed a great deal of her legs and breasts. Maressa, watching Rynn's eyes flicker over the photo, felt as warm and self-conscious as if it were her own body he looked at.

Maressa swallowed and turned her head aside. Her gaze fell upon Denise. She alone was not craning to see the pictures or discussing the similarities. She stared at the floor with a glum expression on her face. Later, when everyone trooped into the dining room to eat, Maressa noticed that Denise's face grew even gloomier. Maressa wondered what was the matter with the girl, then noticed that Kenyon was not yet home for supper. Could that be it? She remembered Rynn's statements concerning his daughter's unrealistic expectations. Could it be that Denise thought Ken should always be home on time? Poor girl. With the way Ken loved to talk, sometimes she'd be lucky if he remembered to come home before bedtime. Once he became embroiled in an interesting conversation or argument he lost all sense of time.

Maressa frowned. She loved her brother dearly, and she hated the thought that he might be hurt by this marriage. If Rynn was right, if Denise loved a figment of her imagination rather than the living, breathing, faulty Ken, he would be as unhappy as his bride, if not more so. For a moment, she wavered in her resolve not to interfere. Perhaps when Ken came home tonight she ought to talk to him. Then Maressa gave herself a mental shake. She knew if she tried that on Ken, they'd have a roof-raising fight like the ones they used to have in their teens. Better to leave it alone. Ken only got more stubborn if you argued with him.

They were through with the dessert and sitting in the den enjoying after-dinner coffee when the front door slammed and a loud voice shouted, "Guess what, everybody!"

"Kenyon's home," Denise stated the obvious and turned toward the door, her eyes shining.

Ken bounded into the room. "You'll never believe it! I just got an offer!"

"Of what?" Maressa inquired dryly.

"A job, smart aleck," he retorted, his good humor undiminished. "In L.A."

"L.A.?" Elizabeth repeated, puzzled. "But I thought you wanted to go to New York. The legitimate theater."

"Los Angeles?" Denise exclaimed in a horrified voice.

"Yes, isn't that wonderful? Naturally, I want to

work in the legitimate theater, but you know that's a tough road. Any break will help me immeasurably. I'll be acting, really acting, for money! It's the greatest thing I can imagine."

Ken lifted Denise from her chair and whirled her around. When at last he set her down, she asked pitifully, "But, Ken, you aren't going to accept it, are you?".

"Not accept it!" he yelped. "Are you crazy?"

"But I thought . . . well, I thought we'd stay in Tucson."

"Here? Of course not. I've graduated. As soon as we're married, we'll have to go someplace where I can get an acting job—New York or L.A. This offer is better than anything I'd dreamed of. Just wait till you hear what it is. It's a movie about teenagers, and I'm playing the part of the hero's jock friend." He rattled on about the opportunity, and the rest of the family enthused with him. Maressa watched Denise slip away to the edge of the room to observe the scene with a pathetically woebegone face. Maressa's heart squeezed in her chest. She was convinced now that Rynn had been correct in his assumptions. Denise had been living in a dream world as far as her future with Ken was concerned. She had obviously believed his acting was a pipe dream, which he would give up after marriage.

Maressa went to her brother and gave him a heartfelt hug. "Congratulations. I know you'll do well."

"Thank you, Mare. You don't often get a chance like this." His green eyes, so much like Maressa's, glowed.

Maressa wished she could share Ken's unblemished happiness. But she was worried about what would happen to his marriage if Denise really didn't want him to act or move away from Arizona. She left the clot of well-wishers and trailed out of the room and across the patio to sit down at the pool's edge, kicking off her sandals and pulling her full skirt above her knees, she dangled her bare legs in the pool. The desert air, cool at night, played on her exposed back. The water before her was dark and soothing. Gratefully she let any thoughts of Denise and Kenyon slip away. Musing idly, she found that the image of a tall man with dark hair and silver-gray eyes had drifted into her mind. Maressa smiled and closed her eyes, giving herself up to the dream.

A shoe scraped on the pavement close by, and Maressa's head jerked up. Her vision had materialized beside her.

"Rynn!" She scrambled to her feet.

His eyes glittered like chips of ice in the pale moonlight. "Maressa. I wondered what had happened to you. You left the celebration early."

"I was thinking about something."

"What?"

"Uh...Denise and Ken, actually."

"You, too?"

"Yes. I was thinking that what you said was probably true. Denise didn't seem happy tonight about moving to Los Angeles."

"No." His face fell. "I'm afraid she's in for a heartbreak." He moved away and sat on the end of one of the lounge chairs, propping his elbows on his knees and resting his chin on his clasped hands. Staring into the water, he went on, "That's the most difficult thing about being a parent. It's not the hard work—the struggling to support them while trying to make the time to be a good parent. It's knowing that you can't change things for them. You can't make everything nice so your baby won't get hurt. I thought a lot about what you said this morning."

Impulsively Maressa sat down beside him and put a hand on his arm. "Oh, no, please, I spoke out of turn. Who am I to tell a father how to act with his daughter?"

"No, you're very wise—wise beyond your years, I'd say. You were right. I can't live Denise's life for her. I've tried to guide her as best I could, and that's all I can do. She has to make her own mistakes. It's the only way she'll ever learn or grow up. I kept her a baby far too long, tried to protect her from reality. I couldn't help her mother or diminish her suffering, so I tried to compensate by making sure Denise never had any worries or pain. It was wrong. Yet here I am, trying to do the same thing all over again."

"It's only natural to want what's best for her."

"I know. But you were right. There's nothing I can do about this marriage, and talking to her only makes her more determined to go through with it. She has to make her own mistakes and learn from them. I can't shield her from life anymore. After our ride this morning, Denise took me on a tour of Tucson and the university campus. I told her then that I hadn't meant to lean on her. It was my opinion that she was marrying too young, but of course it was ultimately her decision and I'd go along with whatever she decided." He grinned at the memory. "Her mouth dropped open a foot. I hadn't realized I was so overbearing."

"Some of us knuckle under less easily than others."

"I take it you're one who doesn't knuckle under?"

"But of course. Who do you think kept Ken in line all these years? Believe me, it was a tough job."

"I'm sure." He stood up and smiled down at her. Maressa extended her hands to be helped up, and he pulled her easily to her feet. They stood close together, hardly a breath apart. Maressa tilted back her head to gaze up at him. Suddenly his gray eyes darkened and his mouth became taut. Slowly the iron gaze slid to her lips, which were slightly parted, soft and beckoning. Maressa's heart began a wild leaping and her fingers were suddenly cold. A crazy feeling invaded her, part fear, part anticipation and part wild joy swelling her chest. She wet her lips nervously.

Rynn's breath came out in a rush and he lowered his head, briefly brushing his lips against hers. Almost immediately he drew back, but Maressa followed him impetuously, keeping their mouths locked together. A shudder ran through Rynn and his arms fastened around her like steel bands, pressing the lushness of her body into his tough, muscled frame. Her breasts were flattened against his rock-hard chest, but Maressa didn't mind. She was conscious of nothing but a primitive desire to feel Rynn's imprint on every part of her. His mouth ground into hers, exploring the honeyed cavity and one hand crept up to her nape, sinking into the silken mass of her hair. Maressa twined her arms around his neck and pressed up against him, mindlessly eager for the further delights his lips promised. Her head fell back, exposing her throat to his fiery rain of kisses. Every nerve and muscle, each drop of blood, hummed at the wild touch of his lips.

"Maressa." Her name was a hungry whisper on his lips. His mouth roamed to her ear, his teeth pricking as his warm tongue soothed. His breath was ragged and searing against her ear as he traced the delicate contours with his tongue, sending shivers of delight through her body. His hands slid down her back to press her even more closely against him. She could feel the hard insistence of his desire, and it inflamed her further. She moved her pelvis against his, and he groaned softly. His fingers dug into her buttocks as his mouth moved down to capture hers again, exploring its sweetness with maddening slowness. Maressa's tongue met his, urging him on.

He pulled back enough to allow his shaking fingers access to the front of her dress. As he unbuttoned the bodice, the straps fell from her shoulders. He folded back the loose sides of her dress, baring her breasts to his avid gaze. "Beautiful," he murmured. He gripped her shoulders, his fingers restlessly massaging them, as he drank in her beauty. Slowly his hands drifted down to cover the pale orbs, cupping their fullness. His thumbs circled the pinkish nipples, turning them hard and dark. Maressa stared at him, made light-headed by the awe and passion in his face. She felt no embarrassment, only pride at his pleasure.

Rynn bent and took one nipple in his mouth, rolling it between his lips, stroking it with his tongue. He took great care arousing it and by the time he moved on to the other nipple, Maressa's loins were melting and eager. She leaned back against his arm, giving him full access to her breasts and the thrusting points of the peaks. She wanted more. She wanted all of him. Maressa grasped his arms, sliding her hands up to his shoulders, then his neck and finally burying her fingers in his hair. "Rynn," she breathed and pulled away slightly. She was about to suggest that they move to her house to continue their love play.

But her voice and motion halted him. As if he had suddenly come to his senses, Rynn stepped back, gulping in air. "Oh, God, Maressa," he groaned, "I'm sorry." His mouth twisted grimly. "What am I doing?" Abruptly he turned and left her, his long stride eating up the distance to the house.

"Rynn!" Maressa started after him, then remembered her open dress and stopped impatiently to button it. It took her some time to find the barrette that had held her hair back, for it had popped loose when Rynn had sunk his fingers into her hair. She finally located it at the edge of the pool and, smoothing back her hair, fastened it once again at her nape. Then she hurried into the den to find Rynn.

Her mother, seeing her enter the room and glance around, said, "Hello, dear. Are you looking for someone?"

"Yes—Rynn. I just saw him come in here."

"Oh, he said he was going to bed and went straight to his room. I'm afraid he must have a headache or something. He looked most peculiar. Rather flushed. I asked whether he'd been out in the sun too long today, and he admitted that he had."

Maressa was stymied. She couldn't go charging into his bedroom after him in front of her family and his daughter. She summoned up a smile for her mother. "I guess I'll talk to him tomorrow, then."

Maressa turned and strolled from the room, wandering aimlessly through the cooling night to her cottage. Her blood was thrumming, and her mind was still numbed by Rynn's shattering lovemaking. Why had he stopped? She couldn't think clearly. Had she done something? Said something? Dazed by the magnitude of her emotions, she slipped into her house and undressed in the dark. Her body was still restless and yearning for Rynn, but in a pleasant way. Maressa crawled into bed and gave herself up to the unaccustomed flood of senses and feelings. Slowly she drifted into sleep.

The next morning Maressa awoke with a smile curving her lips. She bounded out of bed, hugging herself with joy. What had last night meant? What sort of cataclysm had shaken her world? She grinned idiotically at her image in the mirror as she brushed her teeth. She took a long shower, bursting into song as she richly lathered her skin. This bizarre feeling must be love. She chuckled as she turned on the coffee maker and made her customary light breakfast of toast.

She was in love. Imagine that! In love with Ken's fiancée's father. It sounded crazy. She knew that most people would tell her it was impossible to fall so swiftly and completely in love. They would call her emotion an errant spark of passion that would burn out as quickly as it had come.

But Maressa knew herself and she was sure that wasn't true. She was the kind of person who made up her mind quickly and never looked back. Even though she had met Rynn only a couple of days ago, even though there were all sorts of obstacles in their way, she didn't hesitate. She knew she loved Rynn Taylor.

From the moment he had arrived, there had been something between them. She had unsuccessfully tried to ignore it, to deny it, to reason it away. But there was a spark between them—electricity—a fire that had nothing to do with logic or age or appropriateness. Last night it had exploded into passion. Nothing had ever rocked her as that had. She had realized in the blinding, endless moment when he first kissed her that she loved him.

It didn't matter that he was several years older. Maressa had always been mature for her age. Nor did it matter that he was a quiet, sober, almost stern man. She had more than enough frivolity and humor in her own family. Besides, she sensed a definite undercurrent of warmth and fun in Rynn; she was certain that, around her, it would blossom. Maressa had never been one to lack self-confidence, and she felt sure that they could work out any differences between them.

She was also sure that Rynn wanted her. After all, she had felt the full force of his yearning last night. But something had held him back. She didn't know what. Was he unsure of his feelings for her? Reluctant to bed his daughter's future sister-in-law? Too gentlemanly to take advantage of a woman thirteen years his junior? It occurred to her that he might still love his wife. But then it could simply be that he was a very private man and the presence of her family inside the house made him nervous.

Whatever it was, Maressa brimmed with optimism—she could change his mind. But there wasn't enough time to let Rynn work through his reluctance. Denise and Ken would be married in a couple of days, and after that Rynn would leave Tucson. She had to pierce his reserve immediately, which meant she had to come up with a very special plan for this evening.

She couldn't do anything about it during the day; it was Thursday and her television show was being taped. Though the taping itself would consume only a small portion of her afternoon, she would have to spend most of the day preparing for it. It was basically a one-woman show, and Maressa was responsible for even the smallest details. Also, she would have to arrive thirty minutes early to go over the questions with her guest and calm the woman down.

First, Maressa actually had to cook the recipe she would demonstrate on the show. Since there was not enough time to do so during the show, and since the stove she used was merely a prop without power, the featured dish was always precooked and ready to take out of the false oven. Fortunately most of her recipes were simple because her program was aimed at the modern, time-pressured, efficiency-oriented cook.

However, another feature of the show was guiding the viewer through one of the guest's favorite recipes, so she would have to cook that, as well. Maressa took her show file out of the desk in her bedroom and glanced over the two recipes she would use today. She was glad she had already picked up the necessary ingredients. Normally she would have had at least one of the dishes prepared before this morning, but Rynn's presence had interfered with her normal routine.

Since the guest's recipe was the more delicate one, an apple strudel, Maressa decided to fix it first. Less damage would be done to her own wine-and-chicken dish if she had to rush it. Maressa slipped on the cool, comfortable attire she often wore in the kitchen. Her house wasn't cooled by the central air-conditioning system of the main house, using a couple of old window units instead, and when she cooked, the stove created so much heat that the smaller units couldn't cope. It was often stifling after she'd spent several hours putting together dishes for her show. Consequently Maressa had become accustomed to dressing in just panties and a long, short-sleeved T-shirt that reached down to her thighs.

She put on the shirt, poured a tall glass of ice water to drink and plunged into making the dessert. When she'd finished the strudel and put it into the oven to bake, she took a break and strolled over to the window. She wondered what Rynn was doing at the moment. Was he thinking of her? Remembering last night? Did he wish it hadn't happened? Or did he wish he hadn't left?

As if in answer to her thoughts, Rynn emerged from the den door and strolled onto the patio. He was dressed in a dark green shirt of a thin material, casually unbuttoned halfway down, and beige shorts that showed off his long legs. Seeing him even from this distance, Maressa felt a warm glow start in her chest. At thirty-eight, he was in the prime of his manhood, she thought, far too young to be stuck in the staid classification of "father of a bride." He looked more like a candidate for groom. Maressa smiled to herself. If things went as she hoped, perhaps before too long that was exactly the position he would be in.

Rynn glanced around the pool and toward the guest house. He loitered at the flower beds and one of the umbrella-covered patio tables, then retreated into the house. Maressa grinned. Last night Rynn had had reservations about her, but obviously this morning he wanted to see her again. Well, it might do him good to be apart from her today. Let him think about her and remember their kisses by the pool the evening before. Her memory might haunt him more than the reality of her presence. Then tonight she'd make sure he saw her looking her best.

She turned back to the kitchen and started to work on a second batch of dough for the strudel. Though she would describe how to make the dough, she

wouldn't have the time to knead it as much as it required. It was far easier to have another batch ready.
When she was through, she wrapped it in damp
paper towels, stuck it in a large plastic bag and set it
in the refrigerator. After that, she peeled and sliced
the apples she would use on the show, also to save
time on the air. As she worked, she tried to think of
questions to ask her guest, a rather shy, grandmoth-
erly sort who was a phenomenal baker. In convers-
ing with her, Maressa had found that it was a little
difficult to get her talking, but once she warmed up,
she exhibited a dry wit and was full of interesting
and humorous stories. It would be a show that required all of Maressa's interviewing skills, but if she
did it well, Mrs. Greenwald's would turn out to be
one of her best interviews.

Maressa sprinkled lemon juice over the apple
slices to keep them looking fresh, then started on the
chicken dish. She was in the midst of making it, her
hands damp and stuck with the various spices she
was using, when the timer on the stove buzzed
loudly, indicating that the strudel was finished. At
the same time, a loud, high-pitched "Yoo-hoo!"
sounded outside her door.

"Damn!" Maressa turned on the faucet and hurriedly scrubbed her hands. That voice sounded very
much like Aunt Corrie. Corrie was a dear lady, but
the last thing Maressa needed when she was rushed
for time was a visit from her talkative aunt. She
flipped off the irritating timer and opened the oven
door. The delicious smell of baking strudel, which
had been seeping into the room for the past half

hour, now rushed out, filling the air with the sweet-spicy aroma of pastry dough and baking apples. She bent and whisked it out of the oven, smiling at her success. It was absolutely perfect!

"Maressa!" The front door burst open, and her aunt marched in with all the lack of ceremony common to the Gaither family. She was not actually a relative of Maressa's at all, being Lionel's sister, but like her brother, she had taken on Elizabeth Scott's family as her own. Corrie was short, dark and wiry, making it difficult to guess her true age. She rushed at life with a vitality that would have done credit to a twenty-two-year-old. Her tanned face was weathered beyond classification of old or middle-aged. Her dark hair, which was cut short and stuck out in a manner that suggested it had been cut with a pair of lawn shears, had only a single wing of white running through it near the temple. Her face was devoid of makeup, and she wore serviceable jeans and a pale blue, long-sleeved shirt. Thick round glasses perched precariously upon her small, upturned nose. Whatever pretence Corrie had had to beauty, she had long ago given it up in favor of her academic pursuits. She possessed a Ph.D. in mathematics from Stanford and taught three courses at a university in New Mexico.

"What are you doing in here?" she continued, scolding her niece playfully, her tanned face wreathed in a wide grin. "I've been in this house two hours, and you haven't even made an appearance!"

"Hi, Aunt Corrie." Little as she wanted the woman around at the moment, Maressa couldn't help but smile back. She set the hot strudel down on the stove top and came out of the cubicle of her kitchen, arms extended to hug her aunt.

Corrie embraced Maressa enthusiastically, then set her at arm's length to take a good look at her. "My, don't you look beautiful! Doesn't she, Rynn?" She swung toward the doorway, and for the first time Maressa realized that Rynn had accompanied her aunt. He stood immobilized, his eyes glued to Maressa.

She was suddenly, acutely aware of her lack of clothing. The T-shirt exposed practically all of her legs, and her breasts pushed softly against it, the darker circle of the nipples faintly visible through the thin material. Maressa knew that in some ways her scanty attire was more enticing than complete nudity.

"Well, come on in, Rynn," Corrie went on in exasperation. "What are you hanging around out there for? All the cool air will escape." She turned back to Maressa, fanning her face comically. "What there is of it. It's hot as hades in here. What have you been doing?"

"Cooking." Maressa still gazed at Rynn. He swallowed, unable to retreat or tear his eyes away, unable even to speak. With the bright sun behind him, Maressa could not see his shadowed face clearly, but she could tell that his eyes roamed her body and that his chest rose and fell more rapidly than normal. He cleared his throat.

"Uh...I..." His voice came out a croak and he cleared his throat again. "That is, I'd better get back to the house, Miss Gaither."

"When I finish scolding Maressa, I'll be over and we can continue our interesting chat."

"Ah, of course." Rynn backed away uncertainly, then whirled and started toward the house. He walked fast, as if fleeing temptation.

Damn! How could any one woman manage to be that alluring? Rynn cursed his own weakness. He wanted her so badly he felt like a kid again. His palms were sweaty and his pulse was racing.

If only she weren't so young... He simply couldn't take Denise's sister-in-law to bed, could he? He was old enough to have more control. Rynn growled a few well-chosen expletives under his breath as he stalked toward the house. What he needed now was an icy shower.

6

CORRIE PERCHED ON MARESSA'S COUCH and patted the seat beside her. "Now come sit down and let's have a nice long talk."

Maressa, who had been staring at the door through which Rynn had just left, jumped and turned to look at her aunt. Whenever Rynn appeared, she seemed to forget the rest of the world. "Oh. I'm sorry, Aunt Corrie, but I can't. Really. I'm right in the middle of cooking a dish. That's why it's so hot in here. I've been cooking all morning. My show is being taped this afternoon, and I have to finish it by then."

"Oh," Corrie's face fell. "I suppose that's an adequate excuse."

"You'll be here for a few days, won't you?" Maressa felt guilty. Aunt Corrie was really a dear, and she had that same childlike sensitivity that Lionel did. Unlike the more resilient members of the family she could be easily hurt, and Maressa hated to have her think that she was trying to avoid her. "I promise. Tomorrow we'll get together and talk. Okay?" Maressa truly enjoyed visiting with her aunt, who could be witty and knowledgeable. You just had to keep her off the subject of visitors from Mars. Every time Maressa saw her, Corrie was off on some wild new theory about alien visitors. Her biggest disappointment in life was that she had never actually seen one. Maressa liked to think that classified her as merely an eccentric instead of a complete crazy.

"Well, I'll have to content myself with talking to Rynn, then," Corrie sighed and jumped up from the couch. "He seems like such a nice, interested young man."

"Now, Aunt Corrie..." Maressa began warningly.

Corrie flung up both her hands like a captured bank robber. "I promise. I promise. I won't hound him about extraterrestrial visitors...although when I mentioned it, he seemed rather intrigued with the subject."

"He's very polite."

"Not everyone shares your skepticism, my dear. Rynn appears to be a very broad-minded sort who will at least listen, even if he doesn't immediately understand or believe."

Maressa smiled affectionately. "Yes, he probably is. But use some moderation, okay? I don't want him to run out screaming into the desert."

"All right. I won't give him the full treatment." Corrie winked at her niece and gave her a little hug. "Good luck on your show. I'll see you again tonight at supper?" Her voice rose slightly in question.

Maressa nodded. "I'll be there."

Corrie walked to the door and paused on the threshold. "You know, you really do look good. Prettier than I ever remember."

Maressa grinned. "Why, thank you."

Corrie walked briskly out the door, and Maressa sauntered into the kitchen, smiling. Apparently love really did show in one's face. Corrie had noticed a difference in her looks, and she was not the most observant of people. Dreamily, her mind only partially on what she was doing, she finished the chicken dish and popped it into the oven. Then she cleared up, rinsing off the cooking utensils and stacking them in the small dishwasher.

When everything was once again in order, she went into the bedroom to dress for the show. After several minutes of pondering, she chose a navy sundress with a devastatingly bare back, but combined with its short matching jacket, it became a cool, elegant, very businesslike outfit. She dressed quickly and put on high-heeled navy sandals crisscrossed with a multitude of straps. For the television camera she put on heavier makeup than usual and braided her hair into a single long plait, curling it into a knot at her nape. The sleek hairdo made her look older and more professional, she thought.

She added the final touches of earrings, necklace, perfume and a slim gold watch. She wound the watch, checking the time again as she put it on. Good. Right on schedule.

Back in the kitchen she put the cooled strudel on an attractive plate and sealed it in plastic wrap. Hauling out a cardboard box, she set the finished dessert and the other items she had prepared into it, then waited impatiently for the timer to go off. When it chimed, she quickly turned off the oven and removed the chicken. Wrapping the hot casserole in a towel, she added it to the box along with the rest of her supplies. After a careful last-minute check, she picked up the box and carried it outside.

Maressa walked around the main house instead of through it, not wanting to be held up at the last moment by any of her relatives. None of them understood the meaning of timetables or hurry. After placing the box on the passenger seat of her small car, she jumped into the driver's seat and sped off. She drove efficiently and at a much greater speed than she had the other day bringing Rynn out to the house. Within half an hour, she had arrived at the television station.

She carried the box directly into the studio, cautiously stepping over wires and debris. The crew had already rolled her set into place, and Maressa arranged the supplies she would need on the counter top. She put the cooked chicken in the oven and the strudel on the open shelves under the island on which she prepared the food. The wood-grain plywood ran only across the front of the island, which was exposed to the camera. The back was completely open and contained shelves for her convenience. It was the only place she could store anything, since none of the kitchen cabinets were real and hence did not open.

She had to search for the wooden chopping block, which had somehow gone astray during the week, and finally found it in the coffee room. She returned it to the island counter, rechecked her supplies and their positioning, and then, satisfied that her set was ready, she went to the lobby to greet her guest.

She was pleased to find Mrs. Greenwald there, though she didn't like the nervous way the older woman was wringing her hands. "Hello, Anna," Maressa greeted the woman cheerfully, firmly shaking Mrs. Greenwald's tentatively outstretched hand. "It's so nice to see you."

The woman nodded faintly. Maressa noted a faint line of moisture dotting her upper lip and the slight pallor of her skin. Mrs. Greenwald was obviously in the grip of performance jitters. "How are you feeling? A little nervous?"

Mrs. Greenwald looked amazed at her perception and giggled self-consciously. "Yes, I am. I've never done anything like this before."

Maressa placed a hand on her arm and smiled reassuringly. "Don't worry. Everybody's anxious, especially the first time. I still get butterflies right before the show starts. Why don't I take you through the set? It won't seem so scary if you're familiar with it."

"Would you? Yes, I'd like that very much." She looked touched and grateful for Maressa's concern.

Maressa took her into the dim, windowless sound stage and let the older woman explore the set and the overwhelming array of technical equipment to her heart's content. Afterward Mrs. Greenwald's complexion had a touch of color. Maressa invited her into the tiny office that belonged to her producer and there went over the questions she would ask on the show.

"Don't try to memorize your answers or they'll sound pat and you'll get all confused and upset if you can't remember," Maressa said when she finished reciting the questions. "I just wanted you to know what I'm going to ask so that if there's something you don't like, we can throw it out. It takes away the fear of the unknown."

"You're right. I feel much better now." Mrs. Greenwald offered a small smile.

"Great. We'll be on in five minutes. Shall we get settled?"

They walked down the hall and back onto the large stage. Maressa settled Mrs. Greenwald in her chair and fastened the small microphone to the lapel of the woman's suit jacket. Then she sat and clipped on her own microphone. Frank's disembodied voice from the sound booth asked them to check their mikes, and they spoke into them. "Okay," he replied hollowly. "Two minutes."

Maressa felt the familiar clamping of her stomach, the sudden freezing. She glanced through her papers, making sure they were in order and exchanged some banter with the cameraman. She turned to her guest, whom she thought probably needed a last dose of calming. "When Eddy—that's the cameraman—tells us we're on, we have to be quiet. We can't talk until the first commercial. They'll play the opening music and the credits, and the camera will be on me. I'll be standing over there behind the kitchen island. You won't even be seen. After I've chatted a bit and made my dish for the day, I'll come and sit with you. We'll have our interview, and when the next commercial comes on, you can either leave or stay seated and watch our final segment.

That's when I'll do your strudel and give a few kitchen hints."

"I think I'll stay. It's all so fascinating."

"Okay. Great. I'm going over to the island now." Maressa took up her position behind the demonstration counter, and the cameraman peered into his viewer. "Thirty seconds," he announced. "Ten. Okay, we're on."

The familiar music started, and Maressa stood behind the island looking straight into the camera, a pleasant expression fixed on her face. The music faded and the cameraman pointed a finger at her. She smiled radiantly. "Hello, I'm Maressa Scott, and I'd like to welcome you to 'Maressa's Kitchen.' My guest today will be Mrs. Anna Greenwald, who's going to give us a recipe for apple strudel. I promise it isn't fattening. I'll also prepare a quick and easy chicken-in-white-wine casserole and give you a few helpful hints for the kitchen. But first, this message..."

During the commercial break Maressa gave Mrs. Greenwald an encouraging wave and the woman smiled back, obviously growing more at ease. When the camera came on, Maressa launched into describing the preparation of her chicken dish. She talked easily, as if she was speaking directly to her audience instead of into a blank box. Her cue cards rolled along on the monitor attached to the camera, enabling her to remember everything she had to say and do without having to look down or fumble for her notes. Joking and chatting, she finished the recipe and, opening the oven, exchanged the uncooked dish for the finished product, which she then displayed for a close-up.

Another commercial followed, during the course of which Maressa moved across the studio floor to sit down with Mrs. Greenwald. The chairs-and-coffee-table grouping was called "the living room" and provided a homey setting for interviews.

"How are you doing?" she asked her guest cheerfully.

The other woman smiled. "Much better, thank you. It's such a joy to watch you work. You're even better in person! Why, now that I've seen you, I feel as if I can just talk away in front of the camera, too."

"Good. You'll be terrific. I'm positive."

When the camera returned to them, Maressa smiled and introduced her guest, giving a few details about her life and her prowess as a cook. Then she began interviewing Mrs. Greenwald in a conversational way, and true to her words, Mrs. Greenwald performed admirably. She answered Maressa's questions naturally, and her innate sense of humor popped out in many of her answers. Any of Maressa's qualms about her guest vanished, and their interview sped along. She was almost sorry when the cameraman gave her the signal to wind up for a commercial.

While they were off the air, she thanked Mrs. Greenwald, who blushed and laughed happily. Then Maressa made her way over to the cooking island again, and when the show came back on she led the audience through Mrs. Greenwald's strudel recipe. Another commercial came and went. Maressa wound up the show with her usual cooking tips, humorous anecdotes and bits of news concerning food and cooking.

The show whizzed by, as always. The actual filming each week was the least of her work. Preparation took up the most time: digging for hints or interesting bits of history about cooking, finding new and simple recipes to demonstrate, locating amateur cooks and coming up with something different to ask them. Since the show was syndicated and shown all over the Southwest, she often traveled outside the Tucson area to find a cook with an unusual background or style of cooking. And she had to keep abreast of newspapers and magazines to find her "bits." She'd spent more time in the library since she started this show than she had when she was in college. Usually, as soon as one show was over, she began researching material for another.

Next week, however, she had decided to do something different. Knowing that the wedding would be taking up a good deal of her time, she had decided to devote the half hour to the wedding cake. As soon as the day's filming was finished, she said goodbye to Mrs. Greenwald and thanked her again for being on the show. Then she turned to the cameraman to make arrangements for filming her work at the bakery on Saturday.

It wasn't a practical food item to demonstrate, but Maressa imagined that most of her viewers would be curious about what was involved in baking the traditional wedding cake. Also, it would mean less prior preparation on her part and would leave her with more spare time before the wedding. There would still be a lot of work involved after the wedding, since she would have to edit the large amount of footage, but now that Rynn was here, she was doubly glad she had planned the show that way.

Although the cameraman would not be taping when the cake was baking or while Maressa was setting up for the next demonstration, he would still have to be there the entire time. That meant he would spend several hours at the bakery with a minicam, which would make the show much more expensive than usual. Consequently, the manager of the station had refused to do it at first. But Maressa's producer had liked the idea and championed it with the manager, who had finally given in, persuaded by the show's high ratings and profit margin.

Maressa discussed a few points with Eddy, and they settled on a time to meet at the bakery. Then she cleaned up the set, gave the cooked casserole to the manager's secretary, who was a recent bride and set the strudel in the newsroom for the staff. She was thankful that Doug was out on a story, so she didn't have to put up with his pestering. She dumped the rest of the supplies back in the box and carried it out to her car. At last she was free. It had seemed, at times, as if this day would never end.

She zoomed back to the Gaither house, arriving just in time for dinner. Removing her jacket, Maressa dropped it on a handy chair and wearing just the alluring sundress, she entered the dining room. She slipped into her place at the table, where the meal had already begun. As everyone greeted her, she was aware of Rynn turning toward her almost involuntarily. The hunger that he tried to hide blazed from his eyes. Apparently her absence today hadn't hurt her cause a bit, Maressa observed. She tried to maintain an outward calm, although his heated gaze lit an answering fire in her veins. Maressa glanced around the table at the others. Neither Denise nor Ken looked particularly happy. She hoped they wouldn't spoil her scheme for the evening.

"Say, Ken," she began brightly. "Rynn hasn't seen anything since he arrived except the inside of this house and the university campus. Don't you think we ought to introduce him to Tucson?"

Ken perked up at the idea, his blue eyes sparkling. "Hey, yeah, that'd be great. What do you say, Denise? Rynn?"

Denise hesitated. Maressa leaned toward her and said in a loud stage whisper, "Come on, we'll teach your father not to take life so seriously."

Denise smiled. "Okay, but I'll warn you, you deserve a medal if you can manage that."

Maressa pivoted to face Rynn, her green eyes flashing a challenge, "Oh, I've never known a soul whom a Scott couldn't loosen up. How about it, Mr. T? Shall we paint the town red tonight?"

Rynn's gray eyes gleamed. "I never refuse a dare."

Maressa's stomach lurched in excitement. "I'll have to remember that."

Lucille brightened. "Why don't we all go? We'll have a great big party."

Maressa's stomach sank. The last thing she wanted

was her whole crazy family trooping along and spoiling the intimacy of the evening. She would have preferred not to have even Ken and Denise with them, but she didn't think Rynn would have agreed to go without them.

"A party?" Lionel asked dubiously.

"Oh, no!" Corrie protested. "You can't. Lionel and I were looking forward to a game of bridge tonight. If you two go, we can't make up a foursome. You know how Elizabeth hates to play cards."

Maressa silently blessed her other aunt. Lucille's face fell, but Hamilton brightened at the prospect.

"Why, that would be splendid! Always like a stimulating game of bridge."

"Oh, all right," Lucille gave in with exasperation.

Maressa carefully hid all signs of her relief. "That's okay, Aunt Lucille. We'll go another time when you can come with us."

"Where shall we go?" Ken asked.

"How about Lily Langtry?" Maressa suggested.

"Sure. That'd be super."

"You'd like it, dad," Denise agreed.

"What is it?"

"A turn-of-the-century bar," Maressa explained. "Lots of Tiffany lamps and crystal chandeliers, red velvet chairs, that sort of thing."

"But I'm not dressed for a place like that," Denise wailed.

"I'll take you back to the dorm to change," Ken put in reasonably. "Maressa can bring Rynn into town and meet us at Lily Langtry."

Maressa struggled to keep from grinning. Ken was

helping her scheme without even knowing it. She and Rynn would be alone together all the way to and from the bar. And if she knew anything about teenage girls, Denise would take ages to dress and put on her makeup, so they would probably be at the bar alone for quite a while, too, waiting for Ken and Denise to show up. "That will work out nicely. I promise, Rynn, in consideration of your legs, this time we'll take mom's Cadillac."

Rynn chuckled. "I'd appreciate it."

After dinner Maressa hurried to her house to change, promising to return in an hour. She took a foamy bath and washed her hair, then slipped into filmy pale pink panties and a matching half slip. The outfit she had chosen to wear was a simple black satin skirt and belted overblouse that angled in sharply above the breasts to a round collar, leaving her shoulders utterly bare. In the front, just below the collar, three rows of diamond-shaped cutouts accented the bare look. A normal brassiere was out of the question, and Maressa decided not to wear a stiff strapless. Tonight she intended to be all softness and enticement.

She slid a wide gold bracelet onto one arm and fastened matching gold earrings on her ears, then stepped into black high-heeled sandals that flattered her shapely legs. Brushing her hair back on one side, she secured it with a long black decorative comb, then took a curling iron and turned her hair into a mass of loose curls. She reapplied her makeup, bringing out the beauty of her wide green eyes with muted eye shadow and mascara. She touched Lau-

ren perfume behind her ears and on her wrists, then
inspected her image in the mirror. Sophisticated,
with a hint of wildness—it was exactly the look she
had been striving for.

Smiling, Maressa picked up a small black evening
clutch and filled it with the essentials from her
larger purse. Then she strolled back to the main
house, her soft skirt swirling about her legs with a
sensuous swish. She found Rynn waiting for her in
the den, handsome in a well-cut navy blue suit, pale
blue silk shirt and conservatively striped blue tie.

Maressa was gratified to see him straighten and
his eyes widen in appreciation when she stepped inside. He stared and seemed suddenly unable to find
a place to put his hands. Maressa flashed him the
full voltage of her smile. "Ready?"

"Very."

She was surprised by the double entendre, but
said nothing. "Good. Then let's go, shall we?"

They walked through the house to the garage and
got into Elizabeth's white Cadillac Seville. Rynn
stretched out his legs comfortably and watched Maressa back out and turn onto the narrow gravel road
leading to the highway. He was used to being the
driver, not the passenger; it wasn't often that he re-
linquished the position of control. It occurred to
Rynn that, from the moment he'd met Maressa, she
had had the upper hand. Despite her youth, she always seemed self-possessed and in charge, whereas
he was sweating and as nervous as a kid. It was such
a bizarre switch that he wasn't even sure whether he
disliked it or thoroughly enjoyed it.

But he knew he thoroughly enjoyed Maressa. One arm draped across the back of the seat, he turned slightly to watch her. She was looking straight ahead, seemingly undisturbed by his study of her. He realized he'd rarely seen her from this angle. She had a classic profile; her straight forehead, her nose, her lips, her chin, all looked precisely sculpted. His eyes touched her ear, the comb a little above and behind it accenting it seductively. He thought about removing the flat gold earring and sucking the soft earlobe. What would she do, he wondered, if he slid across the seat and did just that? What if he asked her to pull the car off onto a lonely side road and then took her into his arms, hot and panting like any teenager necking in a car? It had been a long time since he'd stretched out across a car seat, banging his shins against a steering wheel and contorting his long body into painful positions just to fondle the softness of a girl's breast.

Rynn wet his lips and tore his eyes away. He was turning into a real lecher. What was the matter with him? He'd never noticed this craving for a young, nubile woman before. It wasn't just Maressa's youth; he couldn't fool himself that it was. No other friend of Denise's had ever raised his blood pressure even a notch or caused him to lose a second of sleep. It was this one particular girl, this enchantress who looked like a teenager in braids one moment and in the next seemed a wise, and experienced woman of the world. It was only this chameleon, this warm, witty, deliciously sexy woman whom he wanted in his bed. He thought of Maressa lying naked on his sheets, wild and wanton, her bright mass of hair spread across the pillow. He thought of her eyes, green and brilliant with desire, beckoning him. He wondered how he was going to make it through the evening.

Maressa glanced over at him and was startled by the simmering gaze he directed toward her. The wheel jerked a little in her hands, and she pulled her attention back to the road. Her pulse was suddenly pounding in her throat. She'd never seen a look quite like that before—burning with such intense desire, yet so rigorously leashed and restrained. It filled her with waves of heat and cold, but her nature was far too spontaneous to lash it down as Rynn could.

"Have you ever just let go, Rynn?" she asked, her bright cheeks and breathless voice revealing how much his hungry eyes had shaken her.

"I don't know what you mean." His voice was colorless.

"What's on your mind?" Maressa prodded, unsatisfied. "I mean, what would you like to do right now?"

"You wouldn't want to hear what I'd like to do right now."

"Maybe I would. Maybe I'd like you to do it."

His teeth sank cruelly into his lower lip. "You don't know what you're saying. You're a child playing with matches."

"Am I?" Maressa shot him a look that was a brief, but unmistakable, invitation.

Rynn sucked in his breath. She didn't know what

she was doing to him. The little witch! She was tormenting him with this girlish game of hers. The ache of his longing fueled his anger and he wanted suddenly, harshly to teach her a lesson, to let her feel the full flood of a man's passion. Then maybe she'd realize how dangerous it was to tamper with it. "Pull off the road," he rasped.

Maressa glanced at him in surprise. There was no mistaking what she saw in his face, the blaze roaring almost out of control now. She made no reply, but turned at the first side road and pulled off onto the shoulder. She stopped the car and faced him, her heart racing with excitement and anticipation and the faintest trace of fear.

"Come here."

Obediently Maressa slid across the seat to him, though normally she would have bridled at the command in his voice. His hands came up and encircled her throat, thumbs brushing against her jaw. "This is what I'd like to do," he said thickly and kissed her hard. His hands slid up to her face, cupping it and holding her still for his fierce possession of her mouth.

As if she would have tried to move away, Maressa thought derisively, her last clear thought for several minutes. His lips were demanding and forceful, pressing feverishly against hers. His tongue thrust into her mouth in imitation of the ultimate invasion of her body that he yearned for. His fingers sank into her silken curls, tangled and caught. Rynn moaned softly against her mouth and his hands clenched in her hair, pulling her even more tightly against him.

Maressa wrapped her arms around his neck and kissed him back with equal fervor. His heat fired her own, and suddenly her whole body was thrumming with desire. She strained against him, half lying across his lap, her body twisting and searching for the hard thrust of him that would ease the burning ache between her legs. She groaned, flung into a fever that was wilder and more demanding than anything she'd ever known. She spoke his name, and it was lost in the searing cavern of his mouth. His tongue filled her mouth, hard and desperate and consuming. She wanted to give to him, to give everything of herself and then more. Never before had she wanted to melt into a man, to meld with him, body and soul, until there was no separateness to her and she was part of him.

He tore his lips away. "Maressa. Maressa." His mouth trailed down her tender throat and kissed her shoulders and the diamonds of skin bared by her blouse. One of his arms went around her back to support her and the other hand spread across one breast, so clearly naked beneath the blouse, rounded and soft, the nipple incredibly hard. She arched up against his hand, seeking his touch.

Rynn was crazy with need and he knew it. He knew he ought to stop. Had to stop. But his reckless, searching hands and mouth paid no attention to his cautioning mind.

Rynn's hand slid down the soft silk of Maressa's blouse and tugged it free of her skirt. Then, light and trembling, his fingers were on the bare flesh of her stomach. They traveled upward until they touched the curve of her breast. His hand cupped the soft, straining mound and caressed its taut peak. He went to the other breast, his thumb tickling the engorged nipple.

Roughly he shoved up the material of her blouse, muttering, "I have to see you." He gazed at her white, full breasts, the darker circles of her aureoles and the puckered, thrusting points in the centers. He closed his eyes for an instant, then opened them again, drinking in the beauty of her form.

The arm supporting her back lifted her, and he lowered his head to taste the succulent offerings. Her scent enveloped him and in the valley between her breasts he tasted the faint bitterness of her perfume. His lips grazed the lush, pillowy softness of each globe, returning again and again to nibble seductively. Maressa writhed and arched against him, her fingers digging into his hair and pulling his head down harder against her. Rynn began to suck one nipple, pulling it deeper and deeper into the hot wetness of his mouth, playing delightful games with his tongue. When Maressa didn't think she could bear it a moment longer without exploding into a million tiny fragments, his lips left her. She gasped at the loss, but then his mouth descended on the other breast and plunged her once again into the dark cave of desire. His name was a whimper on her lips, barely heard, but the whispered sound drove him to a frenzy.

His mouth ran wild down her stomach and his hand delved under her skirt, caressing her thighs and moving between her legs, where her essence lay hot and throbbing, ready for his possession. His arousal was beyond all words; it was all feeling and the driven need for action. There would be no stopping after this, he sensed, and it was that realization that at last gave him the strength to restrain his hunger. He raised his head and pulled in a long, shuddering breath, his eyes closing as if to shut in the ache and the heat.

Maressa looked up, bemused, too adrift in her passion to understand at first what his action meant. "Rynn?"

"I'm sorry." The words burst out of him singly, like little explosions. His fists clenched. "I will not, I refuse to take you like this."

"Like what?" She sat up, dismayed and close to tears. Suddenly she felt embarrassed by her bare breasts and the disarray of her clothing. Hastily she pulled down her blouse and struggled to tuck it in.

"Like a cheap tumble in the front seat of a car."

Hugging her hurt to her, Maressa slid across the seat to the opposite door. "Maybe that's what I am." She struggled against the downward turn of her lips, the aching urge to cry.

"No! Never. You could never be cheap," he ground out. "You deserve nothing but the best—the slowest, most loving, most skillful lovemaking."

She raised her tear-filled eyes to him, the meaning of his words soaking in and washing away the pain of rejection. She smiled tremulously. "If it was you making love to me, it would be the best."

The honest simplicity of her words sent a shudder coursing through him. It was all he could do to keep from pulling her back in his arms. He swallowed. "No." His voice was hoarse with the effort of his restraint. "No. Not the first time."

The first time! Her heart thrilled to his words. That meant he had at last decided to make love to her, overcoming whatever reservations he had had about it. It also meant that he intended it to be more than a one-time aberration. She smiled and he jerked open his door.

"I'm going to drive the rest of the way," he growled. "At least it'll force me to keep my mind on the road."

7

RYNN TOOK OVER THE WHEEL, and they sped noiselessly through the desert evening. Rynn kept his eyes on the road, and Maressa stared out sightlessly at the sand and cactus. For a long time neither of them spoke, except for Maressa's giving Rynn quiet directions. Finally, after her nerves had settled down somewhat, she decided to get an innocent dialogue going. After all, they had the whole evening before them with Ken and Denise; they couldn't maintain this awkward silence.

"What did you do today?" she asked conversationally.

"What? Oh. I swam a little, did some sunbathing. Most of the afternoon—" a grin flashed across his face "—I spent with Aunt Corrie, discussing whether the pyramids were built by superior aliens and if so, did they originally contain electronic equipment to guide the alien ships to earth. I asked her what she thought had happened to the equipment, since nobody'd found any. She said it was highly delicate and had long since crumbled into dust. Apparently these aliens were colonists from a planet that was doomed to destruction."

"Mmm. Probably ran into its own sun. Corrie's planets are always doing that."

"So the aliens planned to immigrate to Earth, hence the colonists and the pyramids to guide their space vessels. Unfortunately whatever they foresaw happening to the planet occurred before the others got off the ground. They never came, and the ones who were here died out."

"I hope she didn't ruin your afternoon."

"No. Actually, after that we had a rather enjoyable conversation about flying. She's a licensed pilot."

"Oh, yes, I'd forgotten about that. So you two had something in common, at least. Corrie can be a lot of fun. Sometimes I think even she doesn't believe half the stuff she says."

"I liked her once I had recovered from the shock. In fact, that's been the case with the whole clan. I couldn't ask for Denise to marry into a nicer family."

"Why, thank you, Rynn. Here I thought you believed we were a bunch of nuts."

"I seem to be remarkably adept at creating the wrong impression."

Maressa smiled and indicated that he should turn right. "There it is. That first parking lot."

Rynn pulled into the lot beside Lily Langtry and parked. The nightclub was a large frame house of pale pink with white gingerbread trim. They abandoned their conversation as they stepped through the ornate front door. Inside, a Gay Nineties atmosphere prevailed. There were several levels, cunningly divided into many small sections to provide an air of intimacy. In the center of the club several couples gyrated on a small dance floor dimly lit with colored lights. Opaque globes on the walls gave off a faint glow, as did the Tiffany-style fixtures hanging above many of the tables. Huge, ornate chandeliers caught and reflected the light. The furniture was all leather and red plush, and a huge marble bar dominated the building.

Ken and Denise had not arrived yet, so Maressa and Rynn found a table far away from the music of the dance floor and sat down to wait for them. They had chosen an intimate, round, high-backed booth encircling a minuscule table. Ferns hanging from the ceiling added to the sense of enclosure and privacy.

A waitress dressed in black fishnet stockings and a short red costume with ruffled petticoats came by to take their order. Rynn glanced questioningly at Maressa.

"A glass of white wine, please."

"And a martini for me."

"Thank you, sir."

The waitress left, and they turned toward each other. There was a moment of silence, and Maressa knew that Rynn wanted to kiss her again. She was certain of it because that was exactly what she wanted, too. Rynn glanced away and picked up the thread of their earlier discussion. "I don't dislike your family at all. Far from it. If anything, I envy them."

"Envy us?"

"Yes—your gaiety, your fundamental eagerness for life. I...lost what little I had many years ago."

"Why? How did you lose it?"

He glanced at her and shrugged. "It's a long, boring story. You wouldn't want to hear it."

"Yes, I would. I've sensed humor and fun in you from the moment we met. I want to know what made you so serious."

"Well, I'm not as somber as Denise makes me out to be. I guess that was the side of me she always saw."

"But you are very contained. Unwilling to let go and have fun."

He sighed. "All right, then. As I told you, I got married at eighteen and was a father at nineteen. My own father died about that time, and I was left with his flying service. I was trying to work my way through college. At first, I was tempted to scrap the flying service, but I couldn't bring myself to do that. So I tried to make a living with it while I finished college. Janet—that's Denise's mother—had to take a job when Denise was a baby. We were always struggling. I was working about twenty hours a day, never got enough sleep. I matured quickly, but it was a pretty joyless existence."

"Even after you became successful?"

"When we were twenty-three and beginning to emerge from the pile of debts that I'd inherited along with the flying service, Janet became ill. With her medical bills in addition to a child, I had to make a financial success of the business. So I put my nose to the grindstone and kept it there. What time I didn't spend on the business, I spent trying to keep my family and home life afloat."

Maressa reached out and took his hand. "I'm sorry. What . . . what happened to your wife?"

"She had multiple sclerosis. It's a degenerative disease. Over the years she steadily deteriorated, and I could do nothing but watch. She grew sicker and more helpless. God, I hated to see that happen to her! She had been so active. She had a job and mothered Denise well, but she was always ready to do more—go skiing or play tennis, anything. And for that to happen to her! To lose her ability to play any sport, then to become unable to take care of Denise or the house and finally to have to have a nurse to do everything for her. For years I saw her dying right in front of me. I've never felt so useless, so helpless. It got to the point that I dreaded coming home at night. Sometimes I wished I could stay at work all the time so I wouldn't have to see her lying there, wasted, a shell of herself. But, of course, I couldn't stay away. I'd go home and smile and talk to her, pretending nothing was wrong. I had to be there when she needed me. I had to be strong for her. And for Denise." He rubbed the outer corners of his eyes. "I'm sorry. I don't usually talk about this."

Maressa's whole being throbbed with empathetic pain. She raised her hand and lightly stroked it over his hair. "I'm sorry. I'm so sorry."

Rynn took her hand and squeezed it, then raised it to his lips and softly kissed the palm. "You're a sweet, kind girl, Maressa." It made him feel even more of a heel for giving in to his desires with her. She was so open, so giving; she had no emotional defenses. The wrong kind of love affair could damage her immeasurably. And a man so much older, so different from her in personality, had to be wrong for her.

Maressa shook her head, smiling. "I just hate to think of you hurting."

He cradled her hand against his cheek. "Fortunately my work with the flying service paid off and I started making good money. I expanded it into a commuter airline, and it kept on growing. But I was away from home a lot, working, and even when I was there, the house was a gloomy place. That's why Denise is shy and introverted. She couldn't invite friends home for fear it would disturb her mother. She had no one to talk to or play with. And between work and taking care of Janet, I had little time for her—and even less ability to give her any joy or happiness. By the time Janet died, both Denise and I were too set in our own patterns to change. I knew nothing but work, and Denise didn't know how to make friends. Neither of us could talk and laugh with the other one. I'd forgotten and she'd never learned."

"But that's all in the past now."

"Once you've established a serious attitude, it's hard to be frivolous."

"Who's asking you to? But you ought to make room for fun in your life. Try some of that young adulthood you never had."

"'Fraid not. The leopard doesn't change his spots and all that."

"Yeah, and you can't teach an old dog new tricks, either," Maressa added with a dash of sarcasm.

Rynn chuckled. "You lack the proper reverence for age and wisdom."

"Oh, and are they here somewhere?" Maressa glanced around as if looking for someone. "I thought we were talking about staying in a rut."

The waitress brought their drinks and they sipped them. Rynn glanced at his watch.

"I wonder what's taking Denise and Ken so long?"

"Now, now," Maressa admonished. "Mustn't clockwatch your daughter. That tends to make them mad."

"Don't I know it," he agreed fervently. "Actually, I'd lost track of the time. I was surprised to see how late it was. Being with you is so...enjoyable." It was a lame word for all the crazy, wild, wonderful feelings she stirred inside him. He couldn't describe how she made him feel—like a young man again, filled with passion and a zest for life.

But the warmth of his silvery eyes spoke his emotions. The color heightened in Maressa's cheeks. She felt his gaze all the way to the tips of her toes. How could plain old gray eyes be so forceful and captivating? She wondered if he had any idea of the effect he had on her. Did he know she'd fallen head over heels for him? Was that why he had held back, not wanting an emotional involvement? Or was it just that he was so used to sorrow that the idea of happiness scared him?

Maressa leaned forward, planting her elbow on the tiny table and resting her chin in her palm. She smiled lazily at Rynn. "You know what? I don't believe you when you say you don't know how to be anything but serious. I've seen all kinds of sparks coming out of you."

Rynn studied his drink, running his forefinger around the rim of his glass. "A momentary lapse."

"No," Maressa replied firmly. "Just a lonely, hungry, very repressed self trying to get out. And I intend to give that guy a chance."

"Really?" He looked up, his smile amused, almost cynical.

"Yes, really. And don't look so smug. Rynn Taylor, you are going to have fun tonight!"

He grinned and saluted her smartly. "Yes, sir! I'll remember that, sir!"

"Let's start by dancing." Maressa took his hand and started to slide out of the booth.

His hand closed on hers tightly, and he glanced with mute horror at the dancing floor. "There? You must be joking."

"Of course, there. And I'm not joking. Come on."

"Absolutely not."

"Too frivolous?" Maressa cocked a mocking eyebrow.

"It's not a question of disapproval. It's a question of ability. I can't do that." He gestured toward the dancers.

"Why not? Anybody can. There's nothing to do; that's the whole point. You do whatever you feel like."

"And if you feel like running away?" But his amused half smile told her that he wasn't really arguing, only delaying to tease her.

Maressa stood up, taking his hand with her. "Come on. Don't be a coward."

He rose with a martyred sigh. "All right. If it will bring you great pleasure to see me make an idiot of myself, who am I to deny you?"

Maressa laughed and led him onto the dance floor, which was jam-packed, flashing with multi-colored lights and pulsating with the heavy throb of the music. Rynn felt like a fool standing there and trying to get into the rhythm of the music, covertly watching the young couples around him for a clue as to what he should do—but his arms and legs and torso had never moved like that! He looked back at Maressa, who was watching him, smiling and sway-ing to the music. She had no trouble moving to the beat. She had no inhibitions, he thought. Her eyes were glowing, and she didn't take them from his face; her expression was a little dreamy, softly sen-suous. Her eyelids fluttered lower. She came closer and he moved toward her. She backed up and he followed. It was a game, a little dance of courtship. He was no longer aware of the couples around them. He saw only Maressa and the smooth sensuous flow of her body. And unbidden his own body began to move naturally in time with hers. When at last the heavy electric pounding stopped, he was left strange-ly bereft and confused.

"See there!" Maressa laughed, coming close to him and slipping her arm around his waist. Rynn glanced around sheepishly and had to smile.

"All right. All right. I'll admit it. I enjoyed it." He edged from the dance floor.

"No! You can't leave now. After just one dance?"

"I've got to get rid of this coat and tie. They're strangling me."

Maressa followed him, warm and tingling inside. She watched his lean, agile hands work at the tight knot of his tie, sliding it open and pulling the ends free. His movements touched a primitive sexual chord inside her, as if she were watching him begin an undressing that would end with him naked. He unfastened the tight collar button and the one below, then shrugged out of his suit jacket. He turned toward her, holding out his hand for hers, and she applauded silently.

"I can't wait to see the rest of your act."

He kissed her hand, feeling suddenly reckless and carefree and young. "You'll have to. I think I'd rather give a private performance."

She thrilled to the provocative implication of his words. "Me too."

They were on their third dance when Maressa glanced across the restaurant and spied Denise and Ken making their way slowly toward the dance floor. Denise's jaw was slack with shock. Maressa hid a smile and touched Rynn on the arm. He swiveled and looked in the same direction. When he saw Denise, he grinned and waved and returned to his dancing. Ken pulled Denise out onto the floor. There was no stupefied amazement on his face; it didn't seem odd to him to see Denise's father dancing with Maressa to the deafening, vibrating rhythms of the latest songs.

When the music stopped, Rynn turned to the

other couple. He shook Ken's hand, and they all
walked from the dance floor to their table, one of
Rynn's arms around his daughter and the other
hand holding Maressa's. "What would you like to
drink?" he asked as they settled down at the table.
He hadn't made a single reference to their lateness,
and again Denise's face registered shock.

"A beer, thanks," Ken replied easily, and Denise
managed to stutter an answer. Rynn signaled the
waitress, and when she came over, ordered again for
all of them.

"How on earth did you do it?" Denise whispered
in an aside to Maressa.

"It wasn't hard. You know, he isn't really rigid or
sedate."

"You could have fooled me."

Denise continued to watch in puzzlement as the
other three chatted. When a slow song came on,
Rynn turned to her, saying, "Ken, Maressa, if you'll
excuse us, I'd like to ask my lovely daughter to
dance." His smile was warm and loving.

Denise put her hand in his, silent with wonder,
and walked with him out to the dance floor. Maressa
watched them with an almost maternal approval.
Ken stretched out his legs and leaned back against
the studded leather booth.

"You know, Neesie's old man is all right," he
commented, using the pet name that he had invented for his fiancée.

"I think so," Maressa agreed.

"You two seem to have really hit it off."

"Uh-huh." At this stage she wasn't about to reveal anything of her feelings about Rynn to anyone, least of all her talkative brother.

"I'm glad. I was afraid he would be real hard-nosed about everything. He thinks Denise is too young to get married."

"Nineteen is pretty young."

Ken shrugged. "Denise is a lot more serious and mature than any of us."

"Ken, you know quietness isn't always a sign of maturity. It could just mean that she's shy."

"Oh, sure. But she'll get over that." He turned from his contemplation of his future wife and her father to shoot his sister a suspicious glance. "What are you trying to say, Mare?"

Maressa lifted her hands. "Nothing. Don't get your back up. I just think that Denise may be more immature than you realize. Do you know anything about her life?"

"Oh, sure. She told me about it—her mother dying when she was fourteen and all that. She had a lonely, depressing childhood." He winked. "That's why I'm so good for her."

"I don't doubt that, Ken. I just wonder if she's had enough experience to know what she really wants."

He frowned. "Are you serious?"

"I...well, she seems to have some rather unrealistic expectations where you're concerned."

"You mean about my acting?"

"Yes, for one thing."

He shook his head. "Yeah, that really threw me last night when she said she didn't think acting would be my career." He frowned. "But, Maressa, surely she must know whether she loves me. I'm leaving Tucson after the play's over. We have to get married now or be apart until she finishes college." His blue eyes turned dark and confused. "She loves me; I know she does."

Maressa's heart ached, and she hadn't the hardness to continue the conversation. "I'm sure she does, Ken." She squeezed his hand. "I'm sure she does."

When Rynn and Denise returned, he asked Maressa to dance and she agreed gladly. After a few more dances, Rynn staggered comically back to the table, one hand on his heart. "Maressa, please, this is too much for an old man." He sank onto the booth seat where Ken and Denise sat nestled lovingly together. "Isn't there someplace where the dancing's more sedate—and quieter?"

Maressa laughed throatily and Ken straightened, then leaned forward enthusiastically. "Sure. There's Santini's."

Maressa groaned, and Denise's face fell dramatically. "Only if you promise not to get up and act out a scene from *Death of a Salesman* like you did last time I went there with you," Maressa told him sternly and explained to Rynn, "Santini's is the place where the drama crowd hangs out."

"But there's only one guy playing a piano. And you can talk to each other without shouting," Ken added.

"Sounds like my kind of place."

Denise said nothing as they rose and trailed out of the quaint building and into the cool evening desert air. Maressa and Rynn strolled to the Cadillac and followed Ken's sporty MG through the darkened streets to a small, plain bar tucked away in a shopping center. Inside, it was smoky and dim. A piano sat on the far side, and next to it was a postage-stamp dance floor where two couples shuffled around to a slow, mellow tune.

"This looks like something out of a Bogart movie," Rynn commented.

Maressa nodded. "I told you, it attracts drama types."

Ken led the way to his favorite table in the corner farthest from the piano. It wasn't hard to claim it; there was only a smattering of people in the room. Several heads turned at their entrance, and Ken waved and called out greetings all the way across the room to his table. They sat down in uncomfortable wooden chairs while Ken went to the bar to order their drinks. It took him some time to return, as he was halted at practically every table on the way and paused to chat a little.

"Hey, Sandy's got a role in the chorus of a road company this summer. Isn't that great?" Ken told them as he deposited a tray of drinks on the table. "She's a terrific dancer."

"How nice. Who's Sandy?"

"The strawberry blonde over there." He pointed to a table. Maressa vaguely remembered seeing her in one of the plays Ken had been in. She happened to glance at Denise and saw that a tight, almost frozen expression had dropped over the girl's face. *Uh-oh*, she thought, *trouble's brewing*. Maressa looked at

Rynn to see if he had noticed, but his gaze was fixed
on her, not on his daughter. Maressa smiled at him,
all interest in Denise and Ken's problems vanishing.

As they sat talking, people drifted by the table, en-
tering or leaving the bar or just dropping by, and all
stopped to talk to Ken. Some stayed only a few minutes, but others pulled up a chair and joined the
party. Beside her, Maressa could feel Denise growing
stiffer and more withdrawn with each new visitor.

Two young men and a girl breezed in the doorway
and paused, surveying the room. Ken waved. "Hey,
Jimmy! Over here!"

The group turned and smiled and strolled over to
the table. "Sit down," Ken urged. "Tell me about
your play. Furnell says you're going to try to put it
on next year."

The three sat down, and one of the young men
launched into a rapid, enthusiastic monologue about
a play he had written. Rynn took Maressa's hand, and
she followed him willingly from the table to the small
dance floor. He turned and pulled her into his arms,
and she fitted against him gracefully. It seemed as if
they had moved together all their lives. It was so natural, Maressa thought, so right. Did Rynn feel it, too?
She leaned her head against his sturdy shoulder and
felt his cheek rest upon her hair. Once or twice she
was sure she felt the brush of his lips on her hair. Maressa sighed with contentment and snuggled closer.

"I don't know about you, but I think I've about
had my fill of young, eager dramatists."

Maressa smiled. "Me too. Ken's a love, but when
he and his friends get together ... well, conversation

with a bunch of fanatics is always a bore. Denise doesn't look too enthralled, either. I wonder if she's beginning to realize what life with Ken will be like.''

Rynn shrugged. ''Would you think me unfatherly if I said that at the moment Denise's love life is the farthest thing from my mind?''

Maressa tilted back her head to look at him, breaking their intimate pose. ''Oh? And what is the closest thing to your mind?''

He chuckled, and the raw huskiness of his laugh sent a shiver through her. ''Don't ask.''

''Why not?''

''You're too young to know.''

Maressa snuggled back into his chest. ''I wouldn't bet on it.''

When they returned to the table, their places had been taken by two newcomers. Ken jumped up to search for more chairs, but Maressa waved him back to his seat. ''No, I think I'm ready to leave, anyhow. Rynn?''

''Sure.'' The glow in his eyes warmed Maressa. She was certain he wanted to be alone as badly as she did.

Denise perked up and reached for her purse, but Ken didn't see the gesture. He went on brightly, ''Okay, you old folks totter on home. Neesie and I'll stay here awhile longer.'' His arm was around Denise's shoulders affectionately and he squeezed her, leaning over to plant a kiss on her head. Denise looked distinctly bored and disgruntled.

As she and Rynn walked out to the car, Maressa thought about Denise. Although she hadn't planned

it that way, the evening might turn out to be benefi-
cial for Denise and Ken, as well. Maybe they'd be
brought face-to-face with their future problems and
have to either work them out or break apart. Whatever happened, Maressa suspected that Denise was
reaching the end of her patience with Ken's gregari-
ous ways.

Rynn took the wheel again, and they started home
through the dark velvet night. Maressa stretched her
legs out and leaned against the door, content to
watch his strong profile. There was no need to talk,
no need for anything. It was one of those perfect
moments in time when nothing else was required
other than to live it and enjoy it.

He pulled the car into the garage and they got out.
Maressa strolled around the house to the patio, Rynn
trailing behind her. She turned as they reached the
pool. "How about a nightcap in my place?"

He knew it was insane to accept the invitation,
just as he'd known ever since that episode in the car
that she would ask and he would agree. He'd been
sane and cautious all his life; tonight at least, he was
going to take his happiness with no concern for the
consequences.

"Yes." His voice was husky. "I'd like that very
much."

Maressa smiled and slipped her hand into his as
they walked across the patio.

8

Maressa unlocked her door and entered the guest-house, Rynn following her inside. He was carrying the coat and tie he had discarded in Lily Langtry in one hand, and he tossed them casually across the back of a chair. While Maressa went to the small rolling cart that served as her bar, he sauntered around the living and dining areas. "It's a lovely little place," he commented. "It looks like you—colorful, yet easy on the eyes—very pretty."

"Why, thank you. What'll you have to drink?"

"Brandy, if you have it."

"Coming up." She took out a snifter and poured his brandy, then fixed an Amaretto on ice for herself.

Rynn stretched with contentment, sinking back on the sofa as she handed him his drink. "Ahh. Perhaps I should devote myself to the idle life."

"You'd be bored to death in a week," Maressa retorted, settling herself beside him. His arm along the back of the sofa was warm against her flesh. She took a sip of her drink and tilted back her head. It rested comfortably on his arm. "You know, even though my family is admittedly eccentric and not averse to enjoying ourselves, that doesn't mean we don't work hard. There's not one of us who's a loafer."

"No? How about a saddle oxford?"

"What?" Maressa stared, then caught his pun and laughed. "Good heavens, I've created a monster."

"Do you work, then? Is that where you went this afternoon?"

"As a matter of fact, yes. I taped my TV show."

"You have a television show?" He looked stunned.

"Yes. It's a thirty-minute weekly thing, and it's shown in four states. It's syndicated."

"My. I'm impressed."

Maressa cast him an impish look. "And well you should be."

"What is it? A talk show?"

"No. Cooking. 'Maressa's Kitchen.'" She briefly explained the format to him.

"I can't quite absorb this. Aren't you awfully young to have a television show?"

"I suppose so. It was really an outgrowth of my bakery."

"Your bakery?" he repeated faintly. "I'm beginning to think you're a most unusual young woman."

"No. I'm just very single-minded. You see, a family like mine has to have *somebody* who's organized and efficient. Out of self-preservation, I started fixing the meals. I found I enjoyed it, particularly the desserts. I got a kind of artistic pleasure out of creating them, the way Ken does with acting and mom with writing. Mom's friends were always begging her to give them her recipes because they loved her desserts. When I was about sixteen, I let them know that I was the one who made all the goodies and that I'd be happy to sell them some. That's how it started."

"It doesn't sound as if you were exactly timid as a teenager."

Maressa smiled. "No. I've never been accused of that. Anyway, before I knew it, I had such a thriving business I hardly had time for school. Then I decided to open a bakery, and eventually that grew into a cooking show on TV."

He stared at her. "You amaze me. How could you cram so much into such a short life?"

"I'm not that young."

"But you look... you're hardly older than Denise, are you?"

It was her turn to stare. "You think I'm Denise's age? But I'm twenty-five!"

"I didn't realize.... That day when you met me at the plane with Denise, you looked like a child."

"Give me a break. I had on jeans and no makeup and my hair was in a braid."

Rynn blinked, clearly disconcerted. Thirteen years. She was only thirteen years younger than he was. It was still a tremendous gap, of course, but at least she wasn't young enough to be his daughter. He knew men who had married women twelve or thirteen or even fourteen years younger than themselves. Nobody thought much about it.

This was crazy. What was he thinking about? Marriage! It was ridiculous. He hardly knew the girl, no matter how much she tempted his senses. And surely she was interested in nothing more than a pleasant affair. Young people today didn't attach the same sort of importance to sex that his generation had. They took love easily and let it go just as happily. She wouldn't, she couldn't, want anything more from him.

And, face it, that was all he really wanted from her. She was beautiful; she was tempting. But once he had her, once his physical thirst for her was slaked, he wouldn't want anything more from her. They were too different, too far apart in age. There couldn't possibly be the companionship and sharing between them that would weld a more lasting bond between a man and woman. He hadn't the time or the interest for a young mistress or child bride, with her demands and emotional storms and insistence on his complete attention.

A devilish voice in the back of his mind pointed out that there had been no lack of companionship or enjoyment of each other this evening. And Maressa Scott seemed perfectly self-sufficient. Would a woman who owned a bakery and had a television show be immature and dependent on him? If he had to be away from her for a few days on business, he couldn't imagine Maressa doing anything but confidently going about her own business and creating her own fun. Perhaps he was wrong; perhaps they could get along. Perhaps . . .

Wishful thinking. That's all it was. Maressa was no doubt like Ken. She needed people and bright lights and action. She would want to spend every night doing what they'd done tonight, but he had no desire to adopt that as a life-style. He would want to stay at home and read or work on some papers; she'd yearn to hit the hot spots. It would never work. Never. They'd grow bored and irritated with each other. Once his desire for her was satisfied, he would see the flaws in her, the shallowness of youth. He wouldn't want her anymore. He'd be free of this aching desire, able to think more clearly. He could start acting his age again, and this whole problem would be in the past.

To make love with her tonight wouldn't be only indulging his sensual side. It would also free him from this obsessive desire. He could go back to being the rational man he knew. And no harm would come to Maressa. After all, she seemed as eager as he, and she was old enough to know her own mind. It wasn't like seducing a teenager. Maressa was sophisticated, had seen some of the world, knew something about life and men. It would be free and open between them; they would be rational adults about it. She would emerge unscathed. After all, kids her age were far more used to casual affairs than he was. They could make love tonight and then, after Denise's wedding, everything would return to normal.

"A penny for your thoughts."

"What?" He glanced up, startled, and realized that he had been strangely silent for several minutes. He smiled faintly. "I doubt they're worth that much."

"Come on, you're not going to slip out of it that easily. What were you thinking?"

"That you're beautiful."

"And young?"

"And young."

"Is that why you stopped last night? Out by the pool?"

He nodded. "I felt like a dirty old man. I thought of someone my age kissing Denise, and I despised myself."

"But I'm not Denise. I'm not her age, not her personality."

"I know."

"And does it make a difference?"

"Oh, yes, it does." He drew in a deep breath and released it, then honesty compelled him to continue. "But even if you hadn't told me your age, I don't think I could have stopped myself tonight."

Maressa's eyes widened slightly, and she leaned toward him. "Rynn."

One hand cupped her neck, and his fingers began a soft, delightful stroking. "The thought of you has haunted me the past few days. Everywhere. All the time. I hardly notice what anyone else says. I do things without paying any attention to them, just to pass the time. All the while I'm thinking about you—your voice, your scent, the way you walk. Your hair." He reached up and pulled out the decorative comb that held her hair back on one side. The curls tumbled down, loose and tangled, and Rynn sank his hands into them, pulling her closer. "I love your hair. I've dreamed of losing myself in it."

He nuzzled her hair, breathing in her subtle perfume and glorying in the silken strands that brushed against his face, clinging to his eyelashes and lips. He wanted her so much it was a deep physical ache inside him, and he knew he would find no peace until he had tasted of her beauty.

"I want to make love to you." His voice was husky with longing, and it melted Maressa inside.

She responded by turning her face to meet his and kissing his lips. His arms went around her, crushing her against his chest; his mouth took hers greedily. Maressa kissed him back with equal fervor, opening to the hot possession of his tongue. Their kiss deepened, lingering. His hands slid up and down her back. Everywhere he touched, Maressa's skin tingled and her blood warmed. His mouth left hers to work its way across her cheek and take the soft lobe of her ear between his teeth. Maressa gasped at this new delight, her fingers digging into his shoulders.

There was too much hunger between them, too much wanting; their movements were jerky and awkward. But neither noticed the lack of grace in their lovemaking. They kissed and twisted and moved and squirmed until they were lying flat on the couch, Rynn's weight pressing Maressa into the soft cushions. His hands went to her waist and moved upward, traveling over her ribs and on to the swell of her breasts. Her nipples were tight beneath his touch, each movement of his fingers making them harder and more sensitive.

Impatiently he tugged off her blouse and tossed it aside. "You're beautiful," he whispered. "Beautiful."

His eyes were glued to the rise and fall of her breasts, and under his gaze they thrust upward proudly. He swallowed. "I want to see you, all of you."

He unfastened the opening of her skirt and slid the clinging material down her legs. Maressa kicked off her sandals and raised her hips to ease his pulling off the remainder of her garments. When she lay naked before him, he gazed at her for a long moment, his eyes drinking in every detail of her lovely body.

"Ah, Maressa." He lowered his head and began to kiss her—hot, sharp little stabs and nips of kisses covering her breasts and chest and stomach. Then his mouth returned to one breast and at last he pulled her nipple into the sensual suction of his mouth. White-hot flames burst in Maressa, and she trembled with the strength of her passion.

"Rynn, oh, Rynn. I want you so. Make love to me. Please. Please. Make love to me."

He groaned and his hands crept behind her, moving down to caress and squeeze her buttocks. Suddenly he rolled off her and stood. Maressa uttered a soft little cry, thinking that once again he was going to leave her. But he did not. He bent and lifted her from the couch, carrying her into the bedroom and setting her down on her bed. Never taking his gaze from her naked form, he kicked off his shoes and whisked away shirt, trousers, socks and underwear in fumbling haste. Then he joined her on the bed, stretching out on his side next to her.

Slowly, savoring each delicious sensation, Rynn ran his hands over her body, cupping her breasts and tracing her nipples with his thumbs, then trailing his fingers down across her stomach and abdomen and slipping in between her legs. He bent to kiss her again, rediscovering her mouth with lips and teeth and tongue. Their tongues lashed and twined, circling and dancing. Maressa clung to him, her mouth yearning to consume him. And all the while his hands continued to play across her body, awakening every sensitive spot and arousing her beyond all reason.

His touch brought forth sighs and moans and whimpers from her, and every sound of her excitement further enflamed his own. With slow deliberation he explored the center of her femininity, his fingers gentle and expert, bringing her ever closer and closer to the brink. Helplessly Maressa stroked his back and shoulders, her hands wild and hot on his skin, urging him on. Her fingers dug in as she writhed beneath him.

There was nothing else—no thought, no inhibition, no regret—nothing but the need driving him. Nothing but the ache growing and reaching within her. Rynn covered her and she opened her legs to receive him. He drove deep, filling the void inside her, and Maressa arched in response. He thrust slowly, deeply and she moved with him, stoking the flames of his passion. She clutched at his back; his skin was slick with sweat, his breath hot and ragged. Maressa buried her face in his neck as he sent them spiraling ever higher, until at last he touched off an explosion within her. Waves rippled through her, and Maressa arched against him. He cried out hoarsely and shook with the force of his own climax. They were fused together in a dizzying instant of time, their bodies alive with pleasure and supremely joined.

Then slowly their senses returned and they became aware of the world around them—the sheets on which they lay, the ceiling above them, the white moonlight streaming in the window—and they separated slowly. Rynn rolled from her, but they remained clinging together, not yet willing to let go of the magic they had shared.

Murmuring drowsy endearments, they drifted asleep. Sometime later, they woke up, arms and legs entangled still, the air cool upon their naked skin. Maressa rose, stretching with lazy contentment. Rynn watched her, smiling. In the dark of the night, there were no doubts, no worries, only the luxurious enjoyment of being with the woman he wanted. They pulled back the covers of the bed and slid between the sheets. Maressa nestled in Rynn's arms while they talked quietly, dreamily, about anything that came to mind, now and then laughing with sheer joy. They talked about his childhood in Georgia and her own unique upbringing in a family full of creative talent and eccentricity. She recounted Aunt Lucille's introduction to Hamilton, one of the family legends. He told her how his father had taught him to fly before he was old enough to drive a car. They discussed his business and hers. And though their conversation stretched into the middle of the night, neither one of them felt the slightest bit sleepy.

"Tell me about your ranch," Maressa commanded, snuggling against his chest.

"It's beautiful." He smoothed back a stray lock of hair from her face and kissed her lightly on the mouth. "I'd like you to see it sometime. There's a row of palms on either side of the drive all the way from the road up to the house. The house is a red-brick Colonial, kind of big and nondescript, the type of thing that doesn't look like it was ever designed. And there's a manager's house, a horse barn, two paddocks..."

"With white fences?"

"With white fences, three rail. It's a hundred acres or so; not anything like a Western ranch."

"It sounds lovely."

"Yeah. I spend a lot of my time there. I think more and more about living there full-time."

"What about your firm?"

He shrugged. "I have very competent people working for me. I've thought about promoting them and sort of retiring to chairman of the board."

"I can't quite see that."

"Sometimes I can't, either. But at other times, I think it would be a relief."

"That's because it's the only place where you relax and unwind. But you don't have to go to Florida for that."

"No? But Tucson's even farther away from Atlanta."

His words warmed her, and she said impulsively, "There might be other options."

There was a short, trembling silence. Maressa

cursed herself for jumping in and saying something like that. She'd always been too quick to speak. Rynn didn't want to hear that. Just because she was the type to fall in love at first sight, it didn't mean he was. If anything, Rynn was a careful, conservative sort who would continue to doubt his feelings even after he'd fallen in love. Intimating a commitment might scare him off.

"Find something in Atlanta that you enjoy doing—besides working," Maressa went on briskly, and the awkward moment passed.

Finally their conversation lagged and they dozed. It was dark when Maressa awoke to find Rynn was gone from the bed. Even though she had known it for only a few hours, already she missed the comfort of his large body in her bed. She sat up on one elbow and peered through the darkness. She heard a thud, followed by a muffled curse, and she smiled. "Rynn?"

"I'm sorry. I didn't mean to wake you."

"What are you doing?"

"Getting dressed. I'm going back to my room."

"Oh." Disappointment sounded in her voice. Rynn came over and sat down on the bed beside her. His hair was mussed, his eyes sleepy. He wore his trousers and had put on his shirt, although it was unbuttoned and fell open to reveal his chest.

"It's not that I want to leave you," he told her. "I'd like nothing better than to lie beside you all night long and wake up in the morning with you next to me."

"Then why don't you?"

He made an exasperated sound. "Maressa! Dearest, be sensible. I can't very well come strolling out of your place tomorrow morning, can I?"

"You mean you're worried about my reputation?" she asked, her eyes dancing. One hand went to his chest, slipping between the edges of the open shirt and twining idly in the hair on his chest.

"Don't be difficult. How would it look to your parents? I mean, I'm their guest and the father of the girl their son is about to marry."

"You mean this is frowned on by Emily Post?" Her fingers kept up their idle movement, slipping across his skin, lightly grazing his hard masculine nipples.

He sucked in his breath. "What are you trying to do to me?"

"Get you to stay here," Maressa replied honestly.

"I'm trying to be sensible."

"I know. Sensible is not what I'm in the market for right now."

His breathing became a little irregular. "And what are you in the market for?" he murmured.

Maressa smiled and leaned over to kiss the skin she had just touched, laving his nipples with her tongue. He stirred and his eyelids fluttered closed. He muttered something unintelligible, then his arms went around her tightly and his weight pressed her back against the bed.

This time his lovemaking was slow and lingering. His hands and lips touched her everywhere until she was burning. She moaned and twisted under his expert touch, raking her fingernails across his bare back. He kissed her deeply, and his hand sought the tender center of her femininity. While his fingers continued their sensual massage, his mouth traced the line of her throat and touched her collarbone, then moved down to take her breast. Heat built in Maressa, building and demanding until she was almost sobbing with need. She sank her teeth into the soft flesh of his upper arm. The sharp stab of pain shattered his control and at last he thrust into her, hot and demanding. They moved together in a sensual rhythm, locked in a world beyond time or space. With each thrust they surged ever higher, until finally they exploded in a blissful unity.

WHEN MARESSA AWOKE AGAIN, it was light outside and Rynn was gone. She sat up, yawning, and wrapped her arms around her bent legs, propping her chin on her knees. A dreamy smile curved her lips as she thought of Rynn and the night that had just passed. If she had ever wondered about her love for Rynn, all her doubts were gone now. Never in her life had she felt anything like what she had last night. No other man had even come close to touching the deep, magical chords within her. She felt as if Rynn had delved into her very soul.

Maressa found it hard to imagine that he had kept himself from feeling the same thing, but she knew she had to face the possibility that he had. Or at least that he would deny it to himself and her. She wasn't sure why, but she knew that Rynn had been fighting his feeling for her every step of the way. She must not rush him, she thought, must not impulsively spill out her love for him or even hint at the depth of her emotion, as she had last night. *Give him time and space,* she told herself. He was bound to realize that he loved her.

She bounced out of bed and went to the window, gazing out with high good spirits at the desert landscape beyond. She wondered what it would be like to live in the damp, tree-covered South and smiled to herself. After a long shower, in which she daydreamed until the water began to run cold, she dried her hair and dressed in crisp white shorts and a pink-and-white striped halter top. She let her hair stream loose around her shoulders in a thick, shining fall of gold and made her face up lightly.

Then she sauntered out of her cottage and across to the main house, unable to wipe the self-satisfied grin off her face. Jessie was at the dining table, reading a book as she ate a bowl of cold cereal. She glanced up at Maressa's entrance. "Hi, Mare. What have you got up your sleeve?"

"Nothing. What makes you say that?" Maressa went past her into the kitchen to make herself a slice of toast.

Jessie snorted. "Don't give me that. You've got that look on your face."

"What look?"

"Like you just found the solution to Rubik's Cube or something."

Maressa chuckled. "Hardly that."

"Well, you look mischievous and very pleased with yourself." Jessie was not to be deterred.

"Whatever you say," Maressa replied airily, but-tering some toast and setting it on a plate. She poured a cup of coffee and brought it and the plate to the table.

Jessie flashed a glance of contempt at her single piece of toast. "That's all you're eating?"

Maressa shrugged. "I'm not hungry in the mornings."

"You screw up your metabolism by not eating a healthy breakfast."

"That's healthy?" Maressa countered, eyeing her sister's cereal. "Flavored, sugared cardboard?"

"It's fortified," Jessie mumbled as she put another spoonful in her mouth. "Besides, I already had two eggs and wheat toast."

Maressa groaned. "If I ate like that I'd weigh two hundred pounds."

"Not if you were thirteen and had grown two inches in the past year," Jessie replied reasonably.

Maressa sipped her coffee and took a bite of her toast, then asked casually, "Has Mr. Taylor been in for breakfast yet?"

"I don't think so." Jessie narrowed her eyes and studied her older sister. "Is he the reason you've got that Cheshire-cat grin on your face?"

"Jessie! Don't be ridiculous."

"Who's being ridiculous? You two went out with Ken and Denise last night; this morning you turn up glowing and smiling from ear to ear. Now I know that going out with your brother and his fiancée isn't going to do that to you. So that leaves Denise's daddy."

Maressa grimaced. "I thought you were a computer freak, not a detective."

"Just call me Nancy Drew. Well, tell me about it. What's going on? I hope it's lurid."

"Jessie, come on. Do I pry into your private life?"

"It's not the same. I haven't got one. Come on, Mare, please?"

Maressa had to smile. "All right. But if you say anything embarrassing to Rynn, I promise I'll destroy every floppy disk you own."

"I won't, I won't. Give me some credit. I'm not a cretin like Benedict."

"Benedict is not a cretin."

Jessie waved aside her remark with impatience. "Don't get sidetracked. Get to the juicy stuff."

"Certainly not! I wouldn't tell you that even if you were old enough to hear it. But I will say that I... well, frankly, I'm crazy in love with him."

"To the max! He's gorgeous—in an older sort of way, of course. Does he feel the same way?"

"I think so. He seems to, and yet there's a certain reluctance."

"Why?"

"Oh, I think because he's Denise's father. It does seem kind of a strange situation, with Denise marrying Ken. And because he's thirteen years older than I am."

"That's not so bad. Dad's ten years older than mom, and look how long they've lasted."

"Yeah, but Rynn hasn't had their good example all his life. There's been a lot of sadness in his past."

"You mean his wife dying? Denise told me about that. It's sad but, gee, don't you think that'd make him want to jump at a chance to be happy?"

"It's what I'd do. But I've found out over the years that we Gaithers and Scotts aren't the norm."

"That's the truth. Cindy Martin, one of my friends, you know, came over yesterday afternoon and Aunt Corrie started in with all those weird alien stories of hers. I thought I'd die."

"Hello, ladies." Jessie and Maressa jumped at the sound of Rynn's voice and looked up guiltily. He stood in the doorway of the dining room, smiling at them.

"Hello, Rynn." Maressa wondered how much he had heard of their conversation. She hoped he hadn't been lingering in the hallway long, listening to them. Thank heavens that at least their last few sentences had been about something other than Maressa's feelings for him.

"Hi." Jessie gazed at Rynn with frank curiosity. He had, however, by this time grown accustomed to her family's blunt ways and he ignored the blatant stare. Involuntarily his eyes went to Maressa, drinking in her fresh morning loveliness. They smiled, unaware of how long they gazed at each other. Jessie chuckled to herself. Rynn had it as bad as her sister.

Jessie pushed back her chair and stood up. "I'd better be going. See you around."

"Bye, hon."

"Bye, Jess."

Rynn came forward and sat down beside Maressa, their arms barely touching on the tabletop. His voice was low. "How are you?"

"Absolutely wonderful."

"Same here." His hand covered hers and he squeezed it.

Excitement and happiness bubbled up inside Maressa. "What would you like to do today?"

"Be with you. Alone." Rynn smiled at her, his eyes glowing. This morning, after he had returned to his room, he had lain awake, unable to sleep, thinking about Maressa and what had happened between them. He thought about what little future there was for them and how much more sensible it would be to end the whole thing now, before either one of them got really hurt. He paraded through his brain all the reasons they wouldn't suit and acknowledged their painful truth. By the time he fell asleep he had convinced himself that this morning he would tell her firmly that, no matter how beautiful it had been, the whole thing was a mistake and that it was better to call it off now. He would pull back, deny his eager desire, think with his head instead of his loins. If necessary, he'd move into a hotel until the wedding was over so he wouldn't be subjected to the constant torment of Maressa's presence.

Spirits sagging, he had dressed and gone to the dining room. Maressa hadn't yet eaten breakfast in the main house since he had been there, so he hadn't expected to see her. Her presence at the table had been a shock, and his heart had soared. He'd found himself grinning fatuously and staring at her, pulse racing, mouth dry. He'd wanted to laugh for no reason. It was all he could do to keep his hands off her. Rynn realized that he didn't care about the consequences. He'd worry later, when the wedding was over and he was alone again. But now ... now he was going to take the joy that was offered him. For these few days he would have Maressa. He would forget everything else and be only a man in love.

9

RYNN POURED A CUP OF COFFEE and sipped it. He didn't really care if he ate or not. It felt so good simply sitting there with Maressa, her hand nestled in his, talking quietly. He didn't want to break the mood of the moment even long enough to pour a bowl of cereal. Their conversation was desultory and punctuated by pauses and smiles of sheer happiness. They touched each other with soft, hesitant little moves—her hand brushing against his arm or his finger trailing along the line of her jaw—as if they couldn't bear not to touch and yet dared not, for fear their desire would blaze too high.

"Where would you like to go?" Maressa asked.

"I don't care. You decide. You know Tucson."

Maressa traced the prominent tendons along the back of his hand. "There's the Desert Zoo. Or the San Xavier mission is a lovely Spanish church. They're both outside the city. You've seen a lot of Tucson, haven't you? And the university?"

"Yes. Denise showed me around the other day." He didn't care what they said; he wanted only to hear her voice. He didn't care where they went, as long as Maressa was with him.

"How about Old Tucson? It's a Wild West town

built as a movie and TV set. You've probably seen it in a hundred Westerns. Would you like that?"

"Sounds fine."

"Good. I'll ask mom if we can take her car."

There were sounds of movement in the hall, and Rynn snatched his hand away. He stood up and started into the kitchen to get his breakfast just as Anthea walked into the room. "Hi, Annie," Maressa greeted her sister with something less than enthusiasm.

Annie didn't notice. She sank into her chair with a gusty sigh. "Whoo! I'll be glad when this thing is over. I've never worked so hard in my life. Do you know I haven't had time to go riding in almost three days? What's for breakfast?"

"Whatever you want to fix."

"Oh. I was hoping you'd decided to whip up some cheese blintzes or something."

Maressa cocked an eyebrow meaningfully and Annie sighed, getting up to join Rynn in the kitchen. Rynn returned with his bowl and spoon and sat down next to Maressa again, carefully avoiding touching or looking at her. He ate quickly, saying little. He found it hard to restrain his annoyance at Annie's presence. His irritation mounted when he saw Corrie Gaither crossing the den to the open double doorway of the dining room.

"Hello, Corrie."

"Hi, Rynn. Anthea. Maressa. My, everyone slept late today. Must be tired out from wedding preparations."

"That's the truth," Annie replied from the kitchen. "I'm ready for a break. Thank goodness, I think things are finally in order. Of course, tomorrow should be absolutely chaotic. Weddings always are."

"Where'd you get so much experience with weddings?" Maressa asked, mildly amused.

"I've been a bridesmaid for half of my friends in the past couple of years. That's how I knew all about the invitations and dresses and stuff." She shuddered. "The more I see of weddings, the more I think I'll **elope**."

"Good idea," Corrie agreed, nodding her head. "Saves everybody a lot of time and trouble. I remember when my sister Evelyn got married, our father told her he'd give her the money he would have spent on the wedding, if only she'd elope. Of course, she was marrying Martin."

"That explains it."

Rynn choked on a spoonful of cereal, and Maressa patted him solicitously on the back. "I don't know if I dare ask, but what's the matter with Martin?"

Corrie snorted. "He's certifiable."

Rynn refrained from pointing out the incongruity of that statement coming from someone who tracked the movements of little green Martians. "Why?" he asked mildly, already grinning in anticipation of the answer.

"Well, he's a kleptomaniac, for starters," Corrie said flatly.

"Now, Aunt Corrie, we're not sure of that."

"Then why does everybody lock up all the valuables whenever he and Evelyn come to visit?" Annie asked.

"And why did that beautiful Hummel of mine disappear after they visited me? Then mysteriously come back to me in the mail two weeks later," Corrie added triumphantly.

"It does sound suspicious," Rynn agreed judiciously.

"And he makes bird noises."

"He what?"

"He's a bird fancier," Maressa explained. "He does bird calls."

"At four o'clock in the morning."

"He also keeps odd hours," Maressa admitted.

"He's most peculiar," Corrie concluded, going into the kitchen and pulling out a container of yogurt, her usual breakfast. "Frankly, I've never been able to understand why Evelyn married him."

"He's devastatingly handsome, for one thing."

Corrie spooned in some yogurt and shrugged.

"And he can be quite charming when he isn't making bird calls or wandering around in the middle of the night."

"That's true, but I think it's when he's most charming that he's in the clutches of his kleptomania."

Rynn burst out laughing. "I suppose it would help to be very charming then."

"Quite true. Anyway, you should be thankful that they couldn't come to the wedding. Evelyn had already scheduled a cruise, I think."

"What a relief!" Annie burst out. "He probably would have lifted half the wedding gifts."

"When are you making the cake, Maressa?" Corrie asked, bored with the subject of her brother-in-law.

"Tomorrow. I'm filming it for my show."

"Not today? But what if something goes wrong?"

Maressa waved the question away. "It won't. I've done it lots of times before."

"Well, good. Then we can find some time to chat today."

"Oh. Well, actually, I'd planned to take Rynn out to see Old Tucson today. And maybe San Xavier."

"That sounds nice. I think I'll come along. I haven't seen that place in all the times I've visited Lionel."

Maressa stared, her mouth clamped shut. Trust Aunt Corrie to mess it up. How could she get out of the situation gracefully?

Corrie went on blithely, "Why don't you come, too, Anthea? It'd be a nice break from your work."

"Yeah, I guess it would. Okay, I'll join you. When are we leaving?"

Maressa glanced in consternation at Rynn. It was getting worse by the minute. "Uh..."

"That is, if you don't mind us coming?" Corrie added.

After that, there was no way to get out of it. Rynn smiled grimly. "No. Of course we don't mind. When shall we leave, Maressa?"

"Oh, anytime. Whenever everybody's ready." Maressa gritted her teeth. How could a kid like Jessie be so perceptive, and grown women like her aunt and Annie be too blind to see that she and Rynn were in love and wanted to be alone? It didn't make sense.

It took another thirty minutes for all four to get organized. Anthea offered to drive and Maressa gratefully accepted. Giving Aunt Corrie the other front seat, she climbed into the back with Rynn. Corrie kept up a constant chatter that Maressa had to follow and reply to instead of giving her full attention to the pleasure of sitting next to Rynn. Annie drove with her usual speed and nerve. More than once Maressa saw Rynn close his eyes as they overtook another car or made a turn on shrieking tires. However, they reached the movie town without mishap.

Rynn glanced around the Spanish-looking village and chuckled. "This is definitely familiar."

"It ought to be," Maressa replied.

"Oh, yes," Corrie put in. "It's been used in hundreds of movies. You see that long stone trough? I don't know how many times I've seen Mexican village women washing their clothes in it as the hero rode into town."

Rynn glanced down at Maressa, and when their eyes met his gaze was hot with meaning. Maressa felt the sizzle run all through her and wondered if she'd turned red from the heat. Corrie rattled on about Western movies, while Maressa hoped that the faint smile she'd plastered on her face was an appropriate expression for what her aunt was saying.

They strolled around, then, much to Maressa's and Rynn's amazement—and gratitude—Corrie and Anthea wandered off on their own. Maressa and Rynn clambered up a set of narrow stone steps,

Rynn offering his hand to help her. He kept her fingers laced warmly with his as they continued their exploration. He pulled her behind the corner of a building, out of sight of everyone, and kissed her thoroughly.

"I'm having a hard time keeping my hands off you," he growled, reluctant to release her. "Isn't there any way we can ditch those two?"

Maressa giggled. "I'll think of something. I'm sorry. I didn't know what to say when they piped up and offered to come with us."

"We couldn't have refused, I guess. I like them both. I really do. Some other time I'd enjoy being with them. But not today. Not now."

"I know. I feel the same way."

His hand drifted over her hair and down her throat. "I told myself that if I made love to you, I wouldn't want you so much. But I do. It's worse than ever. All I can think about is you and how lovely you looked last night, lying naked in my arms." He nuzzled her ear and neck. "I want you even more now."

They kissed again, pushing into each other, arms locked tightly around the other. When finally they broke apart, their breathing was uneven, their faces flushed and bright. Maressa stepped back and made a nervous smoothing pass over her hair. "Let's finish looking at the place, then we'll drag Annie and Corrie home."

"Good. You know what I'd like to do after that?"

"What?"

"Go to a motel. Where we're all alone for the

whole afternoon. No family. No wedding. Just you and me."

"And a bed."

"And a bed."

"Come on, let's go find Corrie and Annie."

Maressa took Rynn's hand and they hurried through the mock town, searching for the others. "There they are. Corrie! Anthea!"

Corrie waved. "Hi! We lost you. Where did you go?"

"Nowhere." Maressa shrugged. "Have you finished looking around?"

Corrie stared. "We've just started."

"Oh. Well, let's see the rest of it." Maressa started out briskly, with Corrie and Anthea trailing behind.

"Hey, wait a minute," Corrie protested, stopping. "What's the hurry?"

"Oh. I remembered that I have to drive to the station this afternoon to, uh, go over my plans with the cameraman," Maressa invented.

"You'd forgotten that?"

"Yes—silly, wasn't it? I'm sorry, but we really need to hurry. I have to be at the station by two o'clock."

"Well, sure."

"Okay." Corrie looked puzzled, but made no further protest.

As they drove back to the house at Anthea's usual breakneck pace, Corrie entertained them with her UFO newsletter's account of the most recent sighting of an alien landing in the Utah deserts. When they reached the Gaither home, Corrie bounced out of the car, turning happily to Rynn to say, "Perhaps you'd like to see the photos? They're in the newsletter. They're so clear. You can't imagine. It's the most exciting event in ages. I mean, once people see these photographs, they'll have to realize it's the truth. Come along, you must look at them."

"Well, ah, I wasn't going in just yet." Rynn turned pleading eyes on Maressa.

"Rynn's going into town with me, Aunt Corrie," Maressa supplied brightly, taking the car keys from Annie and hopping into the front seat.

"Oh." Corrie frowned, puzzled. "But aren't you going to the studio?"

"Yes. Rynn was interested in seeing the inside of a television studio. He's never seen one."

"Why, you know, neither have I! I bet that would be fascinating. Maybe I'll come al—"

"Oh, no," Maressa interrupted hastily. "I'm sure you'd be bored stiff. Rynn's just going to pop in for a minute, then he has several errands to run. So you'd be sitting there with nothing to do while I talked to the cameraman."

"Errands! That reminds me. I have some shopping to do, too."

"Rynn has to look at tuxedos, and there really wouldn't be time to do anything else." Maressa linked arms with her aunt, turning Corrie around and walking toward the house. In a low voice she confided, "Frankly, Aunt Corrie, when Rynn asked if he could come along, I got the impression that he wanted some time alone. You know, away from our family. He's not used to so many people around all the time."

"Oh, I see." Corrie's face brightened. "Well, of course I understand. I've always been something of a loner myself," she stated with an unabashed disregard for the truth.

"Good." Maressa patted her arm and released it. "See you this evening."

"Goodbye." Corrie waved.

Rynn smothered an expression of relief and slid into the front seat. A moment later Maressa hopped in, and they blasted off in a shower of gravel. "Thank God!" Rynn exclaimed. "I thought we'd never get rid of them. What did you say to make her stay home? I hope we didn't hurt her feelings."

"She was very understanding. I told her you wanted to be alone, to get away from our big, noisy family." She glanced at him and grinned. "Well, it was the truth. You did tell me you wanted to get away from the family. It just wasn't the whole truth."

"You could have told the biggest whopper in the world and I wouldn't care, as long as it got me alone with you." Rynn ran his forefinger along the side of her face. Dreamily he traced the curve of her cheekbone, the lines of her nose and lips and chin. She kissed his finger as it touched her lips, savoring the slight roughness of its texture. Rynn smiled, his eyes narrowing and darkening. His hand slid down across her throat and onto the ridge of her collarbone. "You're so lovely. I'd like to take you right here."

Maressa laughed a little breathlessly. "Now? It'd make an interesting show for the other cars."

His hand went farther down, exploring her curves through the scant covering of her halter top and shorts. He circled each breast, cupping its fullness, and teased the nipples to perky tautness. He ran his hand down the valley between her breasts and over the bony ridges of her ribs, onto the soft, yielding flesh of her stomach. His fingers roamed her abdomen and hips, moving smoothly, inexorably to the juncture of her legs.

"Rynn!" Maressa warned, her breath catching in her throat. Her words were husky and muted. "You're going to cause an accident."

"Sorry. I won't move my hand anymore," he promised, his hand tight against the soft mound of her femininity. "I'll stay right here."

"That wasn't what I meant. Ah." She sucked in her breath involuntarily. "What are you doing? I thought you said you weren't going to move."

"My hand. I didn't say my fingers." He wiggled his fingers for emphasis.

"Rynn!"

He chuckled and reluctantly pulled his hand away. "Lord, Maressa, you make me feel like a teenager again. I've thought of nothing but touching you all day. I've undressed you and made love to you a hundred different ways."

"Oh, yeah? You'll have to show them to me." Maressa cast him a smoky glance.

He swallowed. When he spoke, his voice was strained, "How long before we get there?"

"I don't know. I don't know where we're going."

"A motel. The first one you find."

"Uh-uh," she protested. "Not the first one. You wouldn't want to stay there."

"Then the first one you approve of. I don't care. I've been waiting all day to untie that knot behind your neck and pull the halter down." He made a lazy circle around one nipple. "Do you know how beautiful your breasts are?"

"The subject's never come up," Maressa replied in a choked voice.

"It will this afternoon. I plan to tell you many times."

"If you keep this up, you won't be able to go in and register at any motel." She glanced pointedly at his lap.

Rynn slid to the opposite side of the car. "All right. You win. I'll be a model of propriety the rest of the trip." He paused for a moment, then added meaningfully, "But just wait till we get to the motel room."

They reached the outskirts of Tucson, and Maressa turned into the parking lot of a large chain motel known for its family orientation. The swimming pool was filled with laughing, screaming children. Maressa looked at Rynn. "You think they'll let us in here?"

"I'll just tell them you're my child."

"Rynn!" Maressa punched him lightly on the arm. "If you don't stop all these cracks about age I'll…"

"You'll what?" he challenged, grinning. "Crack my shins with your trike?"

Maressa's fingers moved to the knot of her halter,

and her voice fell to a husky whisper. "I'll show you just how little like a child I am."

His nostrils flared. "Not yet. Remember? I've got to check in first."

He slid out of the seat and hurried into the lobby. Minutes later he returned, a key clutched in his hand. "Room 251," he told her tersely. "Go past the swimming pool and turn left."

Maressa followed his instructions and parked. As they left the car and climbed the stairs, Maressa leaned toward him and whispered. "This feels highly illicit."

"Never done this before?"

"No. Have you?"

"No," he admitted. "I guess we're a very naive pair."

"I guess so." Maressa paused, then flashed him a wicked grin.

Rynn grabbed her hand and darted up the stairs, dragging her with him. He ran to their room and braked to a sudden stop, twirling her neatly into his arms. Pressing her back against the closed door, he kissed her deeply. When he pulled back, Maressa was breathless, her face flushed pink. With hands that trembled slightly, Rynn inserted the key and opened the door. Maressa backed in with the opening door and Rynn followed, slamming the door shut with his foot. Tossing the key onto the dresser, he reached out to grasp Maressa's shoulders and turn her around.

He took her hair in his hands, running his fingers through the silky strands, then twisting it up off her neck. He slipped the other hand around her waist, letting it rest at the bottom of the swell of her breasts. He could feel her heart thudding against the prison of her ribs. Rynn bent and brushed his lips against her nape, moving so lightly and softly it was like the touch of butterfly wings. Maressa shivered and liquid heat ran down her body to the center of her desire. She bowed her neck, pressing it up against his lips, and he nibbled at the graceful arc of velvet flesh.

Maressa moaned and moved restlessly, her whole body blossoming in a welcome ache. Rynn let her hair spill down over his face and head, enveloping him in its fragrant softness, as he continued to kiss the back of her neck.

Maressa's response to him was so swift it almost embarrassed her. Her breasts swelled, her loins seemed to melt, and she knew a sharp, demanding desire for more. She moved her hips, beckoning him, and he did not deny her. His hand came down and cupped her femininity, pressing upward, both soothing the ache and increasing it further. As he worked his magic there, his lips still roamed her neck, magnifying the arousing movement of his fingers until it seemed almost too much to bear.

The way he held her, with her back pressed against his front, her hands could not caress him as they longed to. Yet there was a kind of excitement in the frustration of her need, a titillation in knowing that he controlled her passion.

Finally he released her, raising his hands to undo the knot that fastened her halter. He let the two sides fall, and turned her around to face him. The cloth slid down to the creamy tops of her breasts, exposing only a little of their gentle swell. Rynn grasped the ends of the cloth and slowly tugged it down, so that the cloth inched across her skin. The delicate rub of the material left Maressa throbbing for his touch.

She unfastened her shorts and quickly skinned out of them, eager to feel his hands all over her. She started to pull off her flimsy panties, but Rynn stopped her. His hands traveled down her legs as he pulled the panties off with incredible slowness, and Maressa's flesh tingled wherever he touched her. She was alive and quivering with longing, her nerves sensitized to his slightest touch.

He straightened and moved forward. Taking her in his arms, he kissed her again and again, consuming her with his hot, ardent mouth. Maressa moaned and tugged his shirt free from the waistband of his trousers, rolling it up to touch his sleek skin.

Rynn kissed her throat, then moved downward, his lips caressing her body everywhere until at last he knelt before her. Again his mouth went to work, this time at the very core of her desire. Maressa stiffened, electricity sizzling throughout her. His tongue was a whip of velvet, and he dug his fingers into her buttocks, holding her prisoner to his delightful torment. Maressa shoved her hand into his thick hair, clinging, as she shook in a convulsion of pleasure and cried out.

Her knees were like butter, and she thought she would have fallen if it were not for his strong arms holding her. Rynn stood and lifted her up to carry her to the bed. Maressa lay back and smiled up at him dreamily. She felt replete with a sweet lassitude and quiet love. She held up her hands to him. "Come here. Let me return the favor."

Rynn jerked his shirt off over his head and quickly divested himself of the rest of his clothes, then came to kneel beside her on the bed. Maressa reached up and caressed his hard chest, her hands sliding down his sides to his lean hips and thighs. As he had done, she loved him with her hands and mouth, enticing him to the heights of pleasure until he groaned and pulled her under him with something close to desperation. She parted her legs to receive him, and they began the slow, pulsating dance, building to a final shattering zenith. For one brief, delicious moment they clung together, suspended, beyond time and all reality.

Softly, slowly, they floated back down to earth. Rynn eased his weight from her, but they still lay wrapped in each other's arms. "I wish we didn't have to go back," Rynn murmured.

"Me too. Maybe we won't."

He smiled and smoothed his hand down her hair. He wanted to tell her he loved her. He wanted to tell her a thousand things, none of them wise or reasonable. But he knew it was an impossible situation; he would only make it worse by spouting out his feelings. All they could do was live the moment, curled up here in their own brief, lovely, private world.

10

WHEN THEY ARRIVED HOME, there was barely time to retire to their respective rooms and dress for the wedding rehearsal and the dinner following it. Maressa wasn't in the wedding party and so had no role at the rehearsal tonight, but as a member of the family, she would be expected to attend the dinner afterward.

She took a quick shower and dried her hair, then pulled it up into a severe knot on the crown of her head. After applying a touch of makeup, she stepped into her summer white suit. The skirt was gathered and the smart jacket was collarless with military-style pockets and bright silvery buttons. The sleeves puffed out at the shoulders, then were gathered back in at the tight cuffs. The jacket was hip length, extending over the skirt and belting around the waist. The bright and summery suit was attractive on her slim figure and created a snappy, sophisticated appearance.

Hurrying into the main house, she found her aunts and the younger children waiting for her. "Where's everybody else?" she asked, her eyes searching for Rynn.

"Ken, Annie, mom, dad and Rynn went on ahead

to the church. They didn't want to be late since they're in the rehearsal. Annie said you could follow with us."

"Okay then, everybody up. I'm ready to roll."

"Yes, just a moment, dear," Lucille said, fussing with an earring. "I can't get this stupid thing to hang right."

"They're too heavy," her husband stated, glancing at the large gold disks. "By this evening your earlobes will be down to your elbows."

Lucille shot him a withering look, but everyone else smothered their grins. "There!" Lucille stepped back two steps to admire her reflection. She was clothed, as usual, in a devastatingly simple designer creation. It was black with large white polka dots spattered across it and, with her bright blond hair and still-lovely complexion, it was a perfect choice.

"You look gorgeous," Maressa assured her honestly.

"Yes, my dear," Hamilton added judiciously. "Quite charming. You shouldn't outshine the bride, you know."

"You're a sweetie," Lucille told him. "A liar, but sweet. Be sure to stay that way."

Maressa loaded them all into Hamilton's Mercedes, and they drove to the church. The rehearsal had already begun when they slipped in the back and sat down quietly. The minister and Ken, with four young men lined up behind him, waited at the nave of the church. Anthea stood in the foyer, directing traffic. She pointed to the first bridesmaid who started off down the aisle with measured steps.

Maressa watched the other three girls follow her at regular intervals, Denise standing in for the maid of honor to satisfy an old superstition that it was bad luck for the bride to play herself in the rehearsal. Maressa paid them little attention. She was waiting only to see Rynn. At last, the nervous little flower girl came down the aisle, pretending to scatter petals. Behind her appeared the maid of honor, her hand curved around Rynn's arm. He was dressed in a tailored silk suit of charcoal gray, looking trim and incredibly handsome. Maressa's heart swelled and hammered inside her chest. Unshed tears stung her eyes. Her love for him was so great it seemed almost too much to contain. She thought she might fly into pieces from the sheer force of it.

The rehearsal went off smoothly, though Maressa noticed that Denise looked pale and strained. She shrugged mentally; all brides were under a lot of pressure. Still, the sight of Denise's hands constantly clenching and unclenching, moving and lacing while she stood beside the altar made Maressa a trifle uneasy. When the rehearsal ended, Rynn came over to where Maressa sat and she dismissed the thought of Denise's anxiety from her mind.

"It went beautifully," Maressa told him gaily, letting her eyes speak her joy at being with him.

He smiled and gave a vague nod to Ben and Jessie beside her. "I just hope it goes off okay tomorrow. Denise is a nervous wreck."

There was a small silence. Jessie punched Ben on the knee. "Come on, let's go see mom and dad."

"What for?" Ben protested, but Jessie made no

answer, simply took his hand and yanked him to his feet. He trailed out of the pew behind her, muttering his discontent at her treatment.

Maressa smiled. "Thank heavens for Jessie. I never realized how sensitive she is until today."

"And I never realized how hard it was to be alone with someone. Sometimes I think your family is entirely too big."

"And too close," Maressa agreed.

"Ken's taking Denise to the restaurant where the rehearsal dinner is, so I'm driving her car. Care to come with me?"

"Terrific." Maressa rose with alacrity, and they strolled out of the church and across the street to Denise's small silver Honda.

On the way to the restaurant, Rynn held her hand. Maressa leaned back against the seat and smiled. She felt warm and content, yet there was a fizz of excitement in her veins, as well. Once or twice Rynn put her hand to his lips and kissed it lightly. Maressa refused to let herself think about what would happen after tomorrow.

The dinner was being held in a private room of a fashionable steak house. The dinner was excellent and ended with coffee and the cheesecake for which the restaurant was duly famous. Rynn and Maressa managed to sit together, though not alone, and they talked and laughed throughout the meal, oblivious to the others in the room. However, when they were almost finished with dessert, Maressa became aware of a quiet but definitely acrimonious buzz on the far side of the room. Surprised, she glanced over and saw that all the heads were turning to face the same direction. Ken was talking to Denise, his hands gesturing in their usual flamboyant way, while Denise listened with a set, white face, her mouth taut with anger.

"Uh-oh," Maressa said in a low voice and Rynn sighed, frowning.

Denise's eyes snapped and her voice rose almost hysterically, "No, I absolutely won't do it! And if you loved me, you wouldn't ask me to!"

"What does my loving you have to do with it?" Ken barked back, nerves obviously frayed. "This job is an opportunity that might never come again!"

"More important than me and our marriage?"

"It has nothing to do with our marriage."

"It has everything to do with it! I don't want to live in Los Angeles. I don't want to sit at home all day and all night while you cavort around on a movie set and then go out drinking with your new friends."

"Why would I do that?"

"Because that's apparently how you spent your time before I met you. The way you were with all those people we met the other night at that bar, you must have lived there."

"That was before we met. It has no bearing on what I'll do when we're married. Besides, if you acted friendly instead of shrinking away in your chair every time someone came to the table, you'd enjoy my friends, too."

"I can't help it! People intimidate me."

Ken rolled his eyes. "Denise, this is insane. I know

you're shy, but it's something you'll have to overcome."

Rynn pushed back his chair and strode over to his daughter. Everyone in the room busily looked everywhere but at the scene. Rynn reached Denise and put a restraining hand on her shoulder. "Baby, this is not the time to be hashing this out. Calm down. You and Ken can discuss it later."

Denise jerked her arm away from his hold. "I'll talk about it now! There's never any time to discuss it. Ken's always gone, or we're with other people." She swung her tearful gaze back to Ken. "We haven't had a moment alone together in two weeks! I'm absolutely miserable, and you don't even care."

"That's not true!"

She jumped to her feet, shoving back her chair with a clatter. "It is true! It is! You don't love me at all. And I'm not going to marry you tomorrow!"

There was an instant of hushed quiet. Maressa rose and hurried to Denise. "Look, let me drive you to the dorm. You have prewedding jitters. It's natural. All the trauma of the wedding, the decisions and everything... It's very taxing."

Denise whirled. "You think I'm hysterical, don't you? Well, I'm not. I'm perfectly ca-calm!" Her words ended in a wail as she burst into tears and fled from the room.

They all stared, frozen in their seats, faces stamped with astonishment, as Denise rushed out. The sound of the door closing behind her seemed to free them from their state of suspended animation. Turning to one another, they buzzed in shocked disbelief. Ken, too, had been staring openmouthed at the door. He swung around to look at Rynn and started to speak, then closed his mouth abruptly and ran to the door. Rynn hesitated a moment before following him. Maressa was right on Rynn's heels. She didn't trust two men to handle Denise and her shaky emotions; they'd probably only precipitate another shouting match. Maressa sighed as she trotted to catch up with Rynn's long strides. This wedding was turning into a real mess.

Patrons in the restaurant turned to look curiously at the fourth person in a row to rush from the private dining room and across the restaurant. Maressa ignored them and darted out the front door right after Rynn. He turned, surprised. "Maressa! What are you doing?"

"I might well ask you the same thing."

"I'm going after Denise."

"Then I am, too."

"But, there's no need for you..."

Maressa grimaced. "She's your daughter, isn't she? And my brother's fiancée. Ex-fiancée. And she just might need a woman there. Even I'd hate to face Ken and you all by myself. Think how Denise will feel."

"I'm not going to harass her," Rynn assured her impatiently. "Ah, there's Ken." Ken's small blue sports car came roaring around the corner of the building. Rynn ran out into the parking lot, waving a hand. Ken screeched to a halt, leaned across the narrow car and jerked open the passenger door. Rynn bent and folded himself into the low car, and Maressa piled in after him.

"This car only seats two," Rynn protested. Maressa shot him a withering glance and sat down on his lap.

"I'm not that heavy."

"Will you two stop arguing and hurry up?" Ken snapped. "I saw the direction she's headed."

Maressa closed the door. "Surely you can't expect to catch up with her."

Ken tramped on the accelerator, snapping his passengers' heads back. "Wanna bet?"

He zipped down the block and turned right at the end, flying along a wide, empty side street. Rynn shifted Maressa to one side so that he could get a better view, but after one glimpse of the street whipping past, he wished he hadn't. Maressa clung tightly to the shoulder of Rynn's jacket with one hand and braced herself against the dashboard with the other. The blue MG raced over three blocks, once sending Maressa crashing into the convertible top as it took an intersection dip, then careened around a corner. The rear end of the car fishtailed, sending Maressa and Rynn thudding into the door. Rynn's hand scrabbled vainly across the console, seeking a hold, just as Ken took another turn and they went sliding back the other direction.

"Come on, Ken, you couldn't possibly have seen her drive this far," Maressa protested. "Where are you going?"

"Her dorm. She came this way and I'm guessing she went home."

By the time Ken pulled to a jarring halt in front of Denise's dormitory, Maressa's knuckles were white from gripping the dashboard. She opened the door and quickly slid off Rynn's lap. "Why don't I run in and check to see if she's in her room? It'll save time if she's not there."

"Okay. The phones are on the left as you go in. Her room number's 328."

Maressa darted up the shallow steps and through the glass doors of the dormitory. Inside was a wide foyer where several young men loitered, some talking to girls, others waiting for their dates. She glanced around, peeking into the lobby beyond where there were sofas and chairs for the girls and their dates, just in case Denise happened to have stopped there. There was no sign of her. She went to the house phone and dialed Denise's room number. There was no answer. But that didn't mean Denise wasn't there and just not answering the phone. Her roommate was her maid of honor and was back at the restaurant with the others.

Maressa frowned, then dialed 329. A girl answered the phone brightly, "Hi, honey, I'm late, as always."

Maressa cleared her throat. "Uh, I'm trying to get in touch with Denise Taylor."

The girl giggled. "Oh, I'm sorry. I thought you were my date. Denise lives across the hall. Dial 328."

"I did and nobody answered. But, you see, she was very upset when she left the restaurant."

"What restaurant? You've lost me."

She'd done that before she even began, Maressa thought, but answered patiently, "It's not important, really. The point is that I'm afraid Denise might be in her room and isn't answering the phone because she's so upset. Would you step across the hall and check to make sure she's not there."

There was a pause at the other end while the girl considered Maressa's statement. Maressa began to think it would have been faster to have simply run upstairs to Denise's room and checked herself. Finally the girl said, "Exactly who are you?"

"I'm Maressa Scott, Ken's sister."

"Oh. Yeah, sure, I'll check." There was a clatter, a long silence and then the girl returned. "Her door's locked. I knocked and listened against the door, but I couldn't hear anything. I don't think she's there."

"Okay. Thank you."

Maressa hung up and hurried back to the car. "No luck. She's not there," she announced as she squeezed back into Rynn's lap.

Rynn smiled faintly as she settled in. "Any other time, and this might be very enjoyable," he murmured.

Ken frowned and drummed his fingers against the steering wheel. "Where else would she go?"

"She's probably driving around. That would be my guess," Maressa replied. "All her close friends were at the dinner, so she wouldn't be with any of them."

"True."

"She must have someplace where she likes to go," Rynn put in. "A fountain or a park or a building on campus. A favorite place where she hangs out."

Ken's frown deepened. "We usually spend a lot of time at the Student Union Building. Everybody goes there to sit and talk and drink coffee. That's where we met."

"Too crowded and noisy for someone who's crying," Maressa said, dismissing the suggestion.

"There's the fountain in the Fine Arts Building. Sometimes she'd wait for me there. At this time of night, there aren't many people around. Denise always said it was peaceful."

"Let's try it."

She wasn't there. They drove through the campus, peering out at all the shady, inviting or peaceful spots. There was no sign of Denise. Ken parked the car illegally and ran into the Student Union to check it out, but he returned without Denise, shaking his head.

Ken drove aimlessly through the university streets for another few minutes as they racked their brains for ideas where Denise might be. "Even if she did drive around for a while, she's bound to stop sometime."

"Yeah, but what if she drove out on a highway?" Maressa put in reasonably. "She could be halfway to Phoenix by now."

"That's true." Ken sighed.

"I don't think so. Not Denise," Rynn argued. "She's not a wanderer. She's the kind who'd want comfort when she's upset, who'd go to safe, familiar places. She wouldn't rush off to a strange city. She'd stick with what she knows. I'd lay odds on it."

Maressa checked her watch. "It's been over an hour since she left the restaurant. Maybe she's back at her dorm by now."

"Okay. Let's try again."

This time all three of them left the car and trooped into the dormitory. Ken phoned her room and when there was no answer, they went upstairs to make sure she wasn't there. As they were leaving, they ran into her roommate, who had witnessed the whole scene in the restaurant. She came to an abrupt halt when she saw them and a rosy flush crept up her throat and face.

"Oh. Hi, Ken. Mr. Taylor. Uh..."

"Maressa."

"Yeah, Maressa. Sorry." She stood awkwardly, biting her lip.

Ken was too much in the thrall of his emotions to be embarrassed. He barged ahead with his questions. "Have you seen Denise?" Debbie shook her head. "Do you know where she might be?"

"I don't know. She didn't say anything to me about...any of this. I don't know what happened."

"Do you know anywhere she liked to go to be alone and think?"

Debbie looked surprised. "I imagine you'd know that better than I."

"I wouldn't count on it," Ken said grimly. "Do you know where she liked to go?"

"Well, there is the rose garden."

"What rose garden?"

"Down the street from her sorority house. You know, it has a big sundial and a pretty white gazebo. Sometimes she goes there to sit, but never at night."

"We'll try it, anyhow. Thanks, Deb."

"You're welcome." She watched the three of them

walk away and, curiosity overcoming embarrassment, she called after them, "Say, what's going on
with Denise, anyway?"

Ken shrugged and sighed. "I wish I knew."

Denise wasn't in the rose garden, although they
walked every path of it and loitered in the small gazebo for more than thirty minutes. Ken rested his
head on his hands, fingers shoved into the brilliant
mass of his hair, elbows set firmly on his knees. He
shook his head slowly. "I don't know what to do. I
have no idea where she is or even why she left." He
turned a puzzled face to his sister. "She never said a
word before about not liking L.A. How could she
think we'd stay in Tucson? Why, the other night she
said she thought I'd give up acting after I graduated.
I don't understand. I don't think I know Denise at
all."

Maressa sat down beside her brother and leaned
her head against his arm. "I'm sorry, Kenny."

"I wish I knew what was going on."

"I think what's going on is that Denise is finally
realizing that reality and her dreams are rather different." Rynn spoke from the other side of the small
round building. He sounded weary, and Maressa's
heart ached for him. Poor Rynn.

"What does that mean?" Ken asked, bridling.

"Just that I think Denise saw you as what she
wanted you to be, not as what you are."

Ken frowned and rose. "Meaning she doesn't love
me at all."

Rynn's eyes were troubled as they looked up at
the young man. "I'm sure she loves you, but I'm not

at all sure she sees you as you really are. I think she's denied parts of your personality because they weren't what she wanted to see."

Ken turned away abruptly. "I'm going to look around the garden again." He strode rapidly into the darkness. Rynn glanced at Maressa. "Was I too harsh?"

"No, I don't think so." Maressa moved across the small space to sit beside Rynn. "Ken has to face the truth. Obviously Denise has serious doubts about the marriage. I don't know how they could go through with it at this point, even if we find her and they talk it out."

"I don't, either." Rynn took Maressa's hand and studied it, running his thumb along the lines of her fingers and palm. "You know, I didn't want you to come with Ken and me this evening."

"I got that impression."

"I was too upset and hurt, too full of anger. I wanted to find Denise and whisk her back home to safety; I also wanted to tan her hide for not coming to her senses before now. She's made such a hash of it all. She's put you and your sister to a lot of hard work, and now she's going to embarrass everybody in your family by calling it off at the last minute. She's hurt Ken deeply. I thought how selfish and shallow she's been, and I wanted to grab her and shake some sense into her as soon as we found her. But I also wanted to hold her and make all her pain go away. It was sad and frustrating knowing I couldn't. In other words, I was as big an emotional mess as my daughter. I didn't want you to see me that way." He smiled faintly. "I want you to admire me, I guess. I wanted our relationship to have nothing but happiness and fun."

"Why? Unhappiness is part of life, too." Maressa gazed at him with wide, clear eyes. "I want to share your hurt, too. Not just the fun times or the sweet love in bed."

Rynn raised her fingers to his lips and softly kissed each one. "I'm glad you came along, anyway. Having you with me has made it a lot easier."

Maressa smiled. "Well, at least you couldn't see as much of Ken's driving with me blocking your view."

A grin creased Rynn's face. "Trust you to make me smile about it."

Maressa leaned against him, and Rynn brushed the top of her head with his mouth. "You're so lovely. Even tonight, I can't keep from looking at you, wanting you. Just having you here with me makes everything better."

"I know it must be hard to see your child unhappy."

"They shouldn't get married; I've always said that. I was sure it was the wrong thing for Denise to do. Yet tonight I wished that she would marry him, that she hadn't discovered it wouldn't work. I want her to be happy, and I feel guilty that her life hasn't been a pleasant one. With all I've given her, I've never never been able to give her what she needed most."

"You can't make a person be happy, Rynn. That's something that comes from inside oneself. You have people in bad situations who always make the best of it and enjoy themselves. And you have people with every opportunity who sit around bemoaning their existence and letting life pass them by."

"I suppose. I'm positive that Denise will be okay, that she'll be able to pick up and go on and someday really fall in love and be far happier. At least she'll have a better chance at it." He squeezed Maressa's hand. "But I can't help hurting for her."

"I know."

"I'm glad you're here."

"So am I."

It took two more hours of cruising up and down the streets of Tucson before they found Denise's car parked beside an all-night pancake restaurant. When he saw it, Ken let out a whoop and swung into the entrance of the lot, leaving an irate driver whom he had cut off honking behind him. "There's her car!"

"How do you know?" Maressa asked skeptically, peering at it. "There must be dozens of silver Hondas in this town."

"With a university parking sticker and a dent in the left rear?" Ken countered.

He parked and they went inside the restaurant. Denise was sitting at a corner booth in the rear of the restaurant. A middle-aged man in a T-shirt and jeans, with long, slicked-back hair leaned against the side of her booth, grinning down at her.

"Who's that guy?" Maressa whispered.

Ken shrugged. "I never saw him before."

They started toward the booth, suddenly uncertain of what they would do when they reached Denise. The man's voice became clearer as they approached. "You ought to be careful, a pretty girl like you out alone at this time of night. Lots of men around would take advantage of it. I'd be happy to drive you home. Make sure you got there safe."

Denise glanced around, a hunted expression on her face. When she saw the trio approaching her, she sagged with relief. "Daddy! Ken!"

"Good grief, he's trying to pick her up," Ken exclaimed. He looked at Maressa. "This is turning into a real farce. I thought things like this were supposed to be a tragedy."

The man beside the booth had looked up, startled by Denise's exclamation. He backed away a few steps when he saw the formidable bulk of Rynn and Kenyon side by side. "Hello, Denise," Rynn responded, his hard silver eyes resting briefly on the stranger, then dismissing him. "Sorry we're late. It took us a while to find this place."

Denise managed a watery smile. Tears glimmered on the ends of her lashes. "I'm sorry."

The man sidled away toward the eating counter. "Well, uh, guess I'll run along now."

"Yeah, why don't you do that?" Ken added in his best street-tough voice. The man sauntered away with an attempt at bravado. Ken sighed and turned back to Denise. She gazed up at the three of them towering above her, and her mouth began to tremble.

"What in the world are you doing here in this sleazebox at almost midnight?" Ken demanded. "We've been chasing all over town looking for you."

"Denise, I think you owe Kenyon an explanation," Rynn added.

Denise scooted as far away as she could on the bench seat, her mouth curving down sulkily. Maressa grimaced and stepped between the men and the table. "This is precisely why I came along. Why don't you two stop acting like aggrieved males? Go sit down somewhere and have a cup of coffee. Okay? I'll talk to Denise."

Ken started to protest, but Rynn laid a restraining hand on his arm. "She's right. I'm sure Maressa will be able to talk to Denise much better than either you or I could right now. Come on, let's sit at the counter with the local wolf." He nodded in the direction of the man who had been talking to Denise earlier.

Ken frowned and hesitated, then finally shrugged. "Oh, all right."

They strolled toward the counter stools, and the man sitting there stood up warily. As he turned and fled to the cashier's desk, even Denise managed a weak grin at his hasty departure.

"Wouldn't you know?" she said as Maressa slid into the booth beside her. "I can't even manage to run away. First I went back to the dorm. Then I realized that'd be the first place Ken would look, so I drove around. I got utterly lost, it was dark and I was scared to death my car would break down or something. When I finally got back to an area I recognized, I stopped at the first restaurant I saw. I came in here for a cup of coffee, trying to decide what I was going to do, and that jerk comes over and tries to pick me up! I mean, I ask you. Here my life is in ruins, and some old pervert makes a pass at me."

Maressa smiled. "Life never seems to follow a good dramatic script."

"Tell me about it." Denise sighed, and suddenly two huge tears welled up in her eyes and rolled down her cheeks. "I've messed everything up. Oh, Maressa, I'm such an idiot!"

"Why?"

"Because...the wedding's tomorrow, and we've gotten presents from everybody and all those people are coming to the church. You're making a cake, and Annie's done so much work on the dresses and everything. The florist, the caterer...everything's ready. And I...I just realized I don't want to get married!" Her voice trailed off in a wail, and her shoulders began to shake. Maressa slipped an arm around her and Denise leaned against her, crying her heart out.

AT LAST Denise's tears subsided. She straightened, sniffling and trying to dry her face with her hands. Maressa dug in her purse and came up with a packet of tissues.

"Thank you." Denise sniffed and blew her nose. "I'm so sorry. Look, I've gotten your dress wet."

"It'll dry. Don't worry. Now tell me what you mean. Why don't you want to get married?"

"It's not that I don't want to. But I've realized that if I do, I'll make myself miserable. Ken, too, no doubt. The past few days I've begun to wonder if I really knew what I was doing. Finally I had to admit that I didn't. Dad was right again, of course."

Maressa hid a smile at her disgruntled tone. "Aggravating, isn't it?"

"Yes." Denise managed a trembling smile. "Dad always turns out to be right. It's most annoying."

"Do you not love Ken?"

"I don't know. That's the stupidest part. I thought I did. I thought I was madly, passionately in love with him. I'm very attracted to him. He's worlds of fun and marvelous in—" She broke off, blushing, and glanced down at her hands. "Well, anyway, the thing is, I'm not sure that's love. I thought it was, but now I...I don't even know what Ken is really like. I wasn't aware of a lot of things about him. Somehow I pictured him differently. I thought he'd change, you know, after we were married. I thought the acting stuff was part of his college life. Once we were married I imagined that we'd live here, close to your family. I'd finish college; he'd get a job. Something regular, like everyone else."

"Little vine-covered cottage and all?"

"Yeah. Pretty dumb, huh?"

"Not dumb. But unrealistic. Particularly with Ken."

Denise leaned earnestly toward Maressa. "I feel like I love him; I really do. When I'm around him I'm on cloud nine...until his friends show up, or he misses a date because of a late rehearsal. Then there's this job in L.A. I don't want to go there; I'm sure it would be awful. I was mad because Ken wouldn't give it up for me. That's why I yelled at him and ran out of the restaurant. I was furious with him. That's why I said I was calling off the wedding. But I didn't really mean it; it was a threat." She sighed. "But as I drove around, I thought about it. I decided that I had meant what I said. It would be stupid to marry Ken, as uncertain as I am about my feelings for him. Maybe I'm too young or naive or too indecisive. I don't know. I'm really confused and uncertain."

"That's no way to go into a marriage," Maressa agreed.

"I'm scared. I'm scared to death of it. Maybe it's just jitters that brides are supposed to have. But if it is, I don't know how anybody manages to get married. I can't face it. I don't want to mess up my whole life. I don't want to do the wrong thing."

"Of course not. No one would want you to."

"I'm such a failure. Your whole family must hate me."

"Don't be silly. We don't hate you."

"They will when they find out I meant it about not marrying Ken. After all the work you've done! What about your cake?"

"Don't worry about the cake. I'll make it, anyway; I'm taping it for my show next week. It's no problem."

Denise groaned. "What about the presents? And the guests who are going to show up at the church tomorrow? It'll be so humiliating."

Maressa snorted. "Believe me, my family is hard to embarrass. If we humiliated easily, we would have disowned several relatives long ago. The important thing is you and what you want to do. You can't go through with a marriage just because it would be a social gaff not to."

"I guess you're right." Denise looked at Maressa timidly and sighed. "I'm such a coward. Either way I feel like I'm copping out."

Maressa patted the other woman's hand. "Look. We'll take care of it for you. Tomorrow, Annie, Lucille, Corrie and I will man the phones. We'll call all the guests and explain to them that the wedding's off. Then we'll get out your bride book and match the gifts with the givers and send them all back. I'll cancel the caterer and the florist. They'll charge the full amount, I'm sure, or close to it, but I know Rynn would rather pay those costs than have you marry when you aren't sure you want to. The bridesmaids will wind up with new dresses. No harm done to anyone."

"Except Ken."

Maressa sighed. "Yes. Except Ken. But he'll be able to take it. He loves you; he wouldn't want you to marry him if you didn't want to." She omitted the fact that Ken was very resilient and always had his acting to help him over any crisis. The idea that Ken wouldn't pine away for her wouldn't help Denise's rather fragile ego.

"I suppose." Denise took a deep breath. "I'd better talk to Ken now, hadn't I?"

"Yes, I think it would be a good idea."

Maressa walked over to the two men. They looked up at her expectantly. Ken's face sagged a little as he read the look on her face. "Bad news, huh?"

Maressa curved an arm around her brother's shoulders and squeezed. "I think Denise meant what she said. Why don't you go and talk to her?"

Maressa watched as Ken walked over to the booth and slid into the seat across from Denise. They sat for a few moments, hands clasped across the table, then stood and walked out. They strolled up and down the sidewalk in front of the building, talking. Meanwhile Maressa and Rynn moved over to a booth and tried to fix their attention on coffee and soggy slices of apple pie. They said little, both of them tired and emotionally drained after the evening's events. When Ken and Denise returned, quiet and sad faced, Rynn and Maressa were quick to rise and leave the restaurant. The four loitered awkwardly in the parking lot for a moment.

Then Rynn suggested, "Why don't I get a hotel room in town for the night? I'll take Denise there, and you two can ride back to the house in Ken's car."

"Sure. Okay," Ken agreed. Denise stepped closer to her father. His arm encircled her and she snuggled up to him, a child in need of comfort again.

"All right. Good night, Rynn. Denise." Maressa would have liked to kiss Rynn goodbye, but the situation was too strange and awkward. A cold band encircled her heart, as if this lack of contact between them presaged something, but Maressa firmly ignored it. Denise needed her father now, and no doubt Ken needed Maressa. He would want someone to listen to his troubles. This was no time to be thinking of her own uncertain relationship with Rynn.

Maressa and Ken walked to his car, Maressa resisting the urge to glance back at Rynn. "Would you like me to drive back to the house?" she asked.

"Yeah, if you don't mind. I don't feel up to it right now."

She slid into the low-slung car and adjusted the driver's seat. Ken flopped into the seat beside her and leaned his head back, giving out a funny half groan, half laugh. "This is so absurd," he said. "Like a 1930s comedy where the wedding's canceled right before it's supposed to take place, but then the right man substitutes for the groom. Only this time there isn't even a Mr. Right waiting in the wings to take over. Just the wrong groom."

"Oh, Ken. I'm so sorry." Maressa placed a comforting hand on his arm. "You want to tell me about it?"

"I guess. You can go ahead and drive, though. I won't break down, I promise."

Obediently Maressa started the car, and its engine came to life with a vibrating roar. She pulled out of the lot and turned toward home, sailing through the dark, quiet streets. "So what happened?"

"Denise told me she didn't want to marry me. I argued a little, but what can you say to that? Finally we agreed that we aren't ready to get married, at least not yet. Denise doesn't want the kind of lifestyle I lead, and I can't be anything but what I am. So I'll go to Los Angeles, and she'll go home with her father. It's not a complete break; we'll write letters. And I'm going to Atlanta to see her when the movie's over. She promised to visit me a few times in L.A., and we'll see how she adjusts to it. Maybe, someday, if it all works out, we'll try another wedding."

"How do you feel?"

"Tired. Confused. Geez, Mare, I thought she loved me."

"I'm sure she does, honey. She's just young and—"

"No." Ken shook his head emphatically. "I don't think she really does. I never caught on to it—I guess that's what she means when she says I'm selfish and wrapped up in my career—but the man she described as the man she loved bore no resemblance to me. I think she loved the idea of getting married and having a family. She was as anxious to be part of our family as to marry me. Apparently she realized that being married to me wasn't going to be what she had imagined." He shrugged. "So she got cold feet."

"I'm awfully sorry."

"Thanks." His smile was faint. "Boy, I thought I had it made when I got that part. I had Denise and a start in my career. It sure has a way of blowing up on you, doesn't it?"

"Not always." *I hope*, she amended silently.

"If you don't mind, I think I'm going to sleep a little."

"Sure."

Ken closed his eyes, and Maressa was left to the darkness and the silence the rest of the way home.

When she pulled up in front of their house, Ken opened his eyes and glanced around blearily. His gaze sharpened as he remembered where he was and what had happened that night. He ran a hand through his tangled hair. "Wow. For a minute, I thought it was all a nightmare."

They got out of the car and went into the house, Maressa's arm around her brother's waist. "Can I do anything for you?" she asked anxiously after she unlocked the door and they stepped inside.

Ken shook his head. "No. I'm okay. I love her, but . . . you know me. I have that nice artistic detachment. Every life experience is grist for the mill. And I have a big break waiting for me in Los Angeles. I'll survive, so don't worry. Go on to bed. I think I'll sit up by myself and think for a while."

"If you're sure..." Maressa kissed Ken on the cheek and stepped back, scanning his face with a worried expression.

"I'm all right, mother," he joked lightly, assuming a smile. "See?"

"Okay, okay. Good night."

"Good night, Mare. And thanks for your help."

Maressa left him, walking rapidly down the hall and out the door onto the patio. She crossed to her small house and let herself in. She turned on the light and gratefully kicked off her shoes, letting out a sigh of weariness. What a night! It hadn't been at all what she'd expected when the evening began. Quickly she undressed and washed her face, then gave her hair a quick brush and jumped into bed. Tomorrow there'd be the awful phone calls to make to the wedding guests. She and Annie would have to get started on it right after breakfast. Then there was her show to tape, for which she was going to bake a cake for the wedding that would never take place! Groaning, she snuggled into her pillow and closed her eyes. Maybe when she awoke the next morning, it would all turn out to have been a joke.

IT DIDN'T.

Maressa arrived the next morning at the breakfast table to find most of the members of her family there. Without exception, they turned to stare at her expectantly. She sighed. Obviously she was the first person to appear who had any knowledge of the outcome of the night before.

"Well, don't just stand there saying nothing," Lucille ordered crisply. "Tell us what happened."

"The wedding's off."

Annie let out an exaggerated moan. "All those invitations!"

"Yeah, well, all those invitations have to be canceled today."

"You mean we're going to have to call everyone and tell them not to come?"

"What else can we do? You want to stand up in front of everyone at the church and tell them that the wedding's off?"

"I guess that'd be worse."

Elizabeth took a last bite of her toast and gave a heartfelt sigh. "Oh, dear, dear, dear."

"Are you about to tell me you have lots of work to do in your office?" Maressa asked.

"What? Well, yes, as a matter of fact, I really must finish this manuscript, you know."

"You weren't planning to work today," Maressa reminded her. "You were going to get ready for the wedding."

"Yes, of course, but now that I've had this unexpected free day drop in my lap..." Maressa raised an eyebrow, and Annie suppressed a giggle. Elizabeth bit her lip and gazed piteously at her daughter. "Really, Maressa, you can't expect me to... It's far too troubling. I couldn't tell all those people that the bride has left my son at the altar!"

"Oh, Maressa, stop teasing your mother." Corrie leaned forward and braced her elbows on the table. "You know she's not going to make those calls. You and Annie and Lucy and I can do it easily. Besides, we only have one telephone."

"Two. There's a separate line in my place."

"Okay. We'll use both phones at once; that means two people at each one. We can do it in relays. Say, thirty minutes each. It'll be a snap."

"There are only three people, not four. I have to tape a show in an hour at the bakery."

"Oh, my heavens!" Annie gasped. "I'd forgotten. You're making the wedding cake for next week's show. What will you do?"

Maressa shrugged. "I'll go ahead and do it. It's too late for me to work up another show. It'll be interesting even without the personal bits about my brother's wedding. However, it is a pain that I have to do it today."

"Don't worry," Lucille piped up. "The three of us can handle it. My voice is practically tireless. Just ask Hamilton. Corrie and Anthea can man one phone and maybe give me a break now and then. We'll have Ben and Jessie look up all the phone numbers for us. It'll go smooth as glass."

"Good. I should be back around three, then I can help."

"I certainly hope we'll have it finished by then," Lucille responded. "But before we let you go, you have to tell us everything. All you've said is 'The wedding's off.' Give us the details. What happened?"

Maressa recounted the events of the night before as she ate a quick breakfast of toast and bacon; the others lingered over their coffee. When she finished, there began the usual long-drawn-out discussion, but Maressa avoided it, rising and carrying her dishes into the sink. She'd have to dress quickly in order to make it to the bakery on time. However, after she came back through the kitchen door, she paused long enough to ask, "By the way, I take it you haven't seen any sign of Rynn this morning?" Several heads were shaken in mute negatives. "Well, when he does show up, uh, tell him I'll be back at three. Okay?"

"Sure," Annie said, looking puzzled. "Say, what's..."

"Never mind. I have to rush. And you'd better find that guest list."

"Okay. But I've got some questions for you when you get back."

Maressa waggled her fingers at her younger sister and swept out of the room. She hurried through the den and across the patio to her house, where she showered and threw on light tan slacks and a cool sleeveless blouse. The bakery was always hot, even with the incessantly running air conditioning, and she had to wear more casual clothes than her usual show attire. Heavier makeup was still essential, of course, if she wanted to look good on camera; she just hoped it wouldn't start to run in the heat. She fastened her wet hair into a cool, efficient braid curled in a knot on the crown of her head, thrust her feet into comfortable shoes and ran to her car.

Maressa managed to arrive two minutes before the cameraman did. She hurriedly swept everything from one of the work counters and set up her materials. Fortunately the bakery had everything necessary for baking and icing a wedding cake, so she hadn't needed to bring any supplies for the taping. Eddy, the cameraman, waited patiently for her to lay things out, then they walked through the first segment of the show, in which Maressa would point out the various features of the bakery.

It was more difficult to remember what she was to say since there were no cue cards on the camera, but a mistake wasn't irreparable when the show was being taped. Whenever Maressa flubbed a line, they just stopped and started again. After the opening portion, Maressa showed her supplies and explained the procedure as she did with any of her dishes. Since the show wasn't live, they were able to cut off the camera during the baking of the cake and during any boring or lengthy segments.

In general, the taping went well; they didn't have to spend much extra time on it. The cake turned out just as it was supposed to, which was a relief. When one filmed the preparation of a dish from beginning to end, there was always the chance that the dish wouldn't turn out right. Maressa's brilliant smile as she showed off the finished product was genuine.

"Tell Lynn I'll be in Monday to work on editing it," Maressa told the cameraman, ripping off her apron and close-fitting cap. That was the real work—cutting and splicing the hours of tapes until they had a concise, interesting, properly flowing show that lasted only twenty-two minutes, the time of her thirty-minute show minus commercials. She smiled at Eddy, pleased and relieved. "Thanks for doing this. Want some cake?"

His eyes widened with horror as he looked at the towering confection. "Are you kidding? How can you cut it up after all that?"

Maressa laughed. "That's what happens to all my creations."

She grabbed her purse and started out the door, waving goodbye to the cameraman. With the job behind her, her mind had reverted to Rynn Taylor. She was anxious to talk to him. Now that the wedding was off, what would he do? He was bound to leave Tucson soon. And where did that leave her? He'd never once said he loved her, or even cared for her. Could it be that he would walk out of her life after today? Maressa didn't know how she could stand that. Yet what could she do to stop him?

She arrived home to find everything peaceful. Jessie was in her bedroom zapping aliens on her small television screen. Annie lay stretched out on the couch in the den watching an old movie. She glanced up when Maressa entered, and gave her a halfhearted wave.

"Hi. How goes it?" Maressa asked, flopping down in a chair beside the couch. "Where is everybody?"

"Mom's still hiding in her office. She doesn't know we've finished. I think Lucille and Corrie are so wiped out they had to go take naps."

"That bad, huh?"

Anthea sighed and shook her head. "I thought handling the invitations was bad, but this beat all. Everybody wanted to gossip! They wanted to know what and where and why. Finally I started telling them I didn't know anything about it; I'd just been hired to do the calling."

Maressa half grinned. "Did you get everyone?"

"Naw. One couple was never home. I'll try them again later. At one house, the babysitter answered and said the people were away on a weekend trip. So that couple wasn't coming, anyway. There were lots we didn't get on the first try, but eventually they either answered or we left a message with some-one."

"Great."

"Yeah. Now all we have to do is repackage all the gifts and send them back."

Maressa made a face. She gazed at the television screen for a minute or two without really seeing the action on it, then asked casually, "Has Rynn been out here?"

"Yeah, he came to pick up his bags. He asked where you were. Say, what is it with you two? Is there something going on here I don't know about?"

"Annie, I hate to tell you this, but there are lots of things going on that you don't know about."

Anthea grimaced. "Come on, you know what I mean. How come you two keep looking for each other? Are you interested in Denise's father?"

"What if I am?"

Annie shrugged. "I don't know. I'm curious, that's all. He's good-looking, although he must be kinda old for you."

"He's thirty-eight," Maressa responded quickly. "That's only thirteen year's difference."

Annie swung her feet down to the floor and sat up. "Say, you really are interested in him, aren't you?"

"I'm in love with him," Maressa answered simply.

"Wow."

"Don't you dare say 'awesome.'"

Annie giggled. "I won't. When did all this happen? Hey, yesterday when Corrie and I went to Old Tucson with you, you didn't want us to go, did you?"

"Hardly."

"Oh, no!" Annie chuckled. "I thought it was weird, you suddenly remembering a job at the studio and then Rynn deciding he had all these errands to run. Geez. I bet you were about ready to wring Corrie's neck when she kept trying to go with you."

"You're a master of understatement. You also haven't told me much of anything. Why was Rynn here? Is he coming back? Did he say anything about leaving?"

"Well, he packed his bags and took them with him. Apparently he's staying in a hotel in town until they leave. He apologized to Lionel and mom about Denise dumping their son and creating so much trouble and all that. Then he asked when you'd be back."

"Is he coming back here?"

Annie shrugged. "I don't know. That's all he said."

"Great," Maressa commented sarcastically. "I guess

I'm stuck here. I'll watch the movie with you and then we can get started on the gifts."

"Don't do me any favors."

Maressa smiled and propped her feet up on the coffee table, settling down to wait.

12

"MARESSA?" Rynn's voice was low and tentative, but Maressa's eyes flew open at the sound of her name. She blinked, disoriented for a moment. The television set was blaring out a rock-and-roll show featuring the latest hits, while Annie dozed on the couch. Maressa realized that she must have fallen asleep watching the movie. It had been a hard day, and last night she hadn't come in till late.

"Rynn." Maressa rose, reaching out to clasp his hands.

He smiled down at her, his gray eyes warm and tinged with sadness. "I'm sorry to waken you. I came out earlier, but you weren't here, so I returned."

"I'm glad you did." She turned off the television with a flick of her wrist, and Annie immediately wakened. She sat bolt upright and stared at Rynn and Maressa with blank eyes. "Annie, Rynn's here. Uh, why don't you get started on the presents?"

"Now? You've got to be kidding. Oh. Yeah." Annie's eyes cleared, and she jumped to her feet. "Sure. I'll, uh, go do that." She hurried out of the room.

Rynn sighed. "I'm afraid Denise has caused your family endless trouble. Annie told me she and your aunts made all the calls about the canceled wedding.

And now the gifts.... Denise should be doing that; it's her responsibility."

Maressa lifted her shoulders in a gesture of dismissal. "I don't think responsibility means too much when your life's suddenly turned upside down." Maressa didn't like the sober lines of Rynn's face, the sorrow in his eyes, so she scrambled for the first topic she could think of to postpone what she feared was coming. "How is Denise?"

"All right, I suppose. She's returning to Atlanta with me. I told her that I'd speak to a friend about getting her a job for the summer. She perked up a little at that idea. I think it'll be good for her, give her a taste of real life."

"Probably."

"We're flying to Atlanta tomorrow morning. I'd planned to go this evening, but when you weren't here, I changed our reservations. I... wanted to see you before I left."

"I see." Maressa's knees felt weak, and she sank back onto her chair. "After you've gone home, you don't plan to see me again?"

The lines around Rynn's mouth deepened. He thrust his hands into his pockets, moving away. "Please, Maressa, don't look at me like that."

"How should I look at you? I'm afraid I've never been too good at hiding my feelings."

"It's not that I don't want to see you again. If I followed my heart, I'd be back here every weekend."

Maressa's head popped up and she turned fiery, furious eyes on him. "And why shouldn't you follow your heart?"

"Denise was brave enough to face reality. I have to be, too. Maressa, I'm not as young as you. Not as carefree. It's simply not in my nature to have a casual affair. I realize that people your age are more open, more free and easy about such things."

"Wait a minute. What do you mean, 'people my age'? You sound as if we belong to separate generations. You're only thirteen years older than I am."

"We're eons apart, I think, when it comes to sexual mores."

Maressa raised an eyebrow. "Exactly what are you saying about me? Do you think I have this sort of fling with every man who comes along? That I run from one meaningless affair to another? Thank you very much! I appreciate your high opinion of me!"

"No! Don't be ridiculous. I don't mean that at all. I just mean that young people are less committed. You have a looser life-style."

"You're digging yourself in deeper," Maressa warned, unable to suppress amusement at his discomfiture.

"Damn it! You know what I mean. You have a freer approach to sex. I don't—I can't—indulge in lovemaking without commitment. I love you, Maressa. The more I'm around you, the deeper in love I get. If I continued to see you, to make love to you...it'd kill me when you left. I can't, darling. Maybe it's cowardly, but I don't want to risk my whole soul. It's better to have the pain of separation now."

Joy shot up in Maressa like a fountain, spraying out and touching every part of her. Rynn loved her!

He loved her. The rest of his words were meaningless as long as he loved her. She faced him, hands on hips, eyes flaming. "You're absolutely cowardly. More than that. You're pompous and bigoted and half a dozen things I won't even mention. It'd be exactly what you deserved if I let you get away with this."

He blinked, startled by her reaction. "Maressa..."

"You know, you've assumed an awful lot about me from the moment you met me. First, you assumed I was Denise's age. Then you decided I wasn't ready for a love affair with you. Now you're assuming that I'm interested only in a frivolous affair, that I have no feeling for you in spite of all the glorious things that have happened between us. You assume I'm promiscuous; you assume I have no commitment to you; you assume I'm a featherweight without morals or deep feelings or—"

"Wait, wait! Slow down. I never said that." The redness of anger tinged Rynn's cheeks. "You're not a featherweight. And I never said you were promiscuous. Maressa, I think you're a beautiful, warm, loving person, more generous and lovely than I could ever deserve. I would never call you loose or shallow. I love you!"

"It's pretty hard to tell that from the things you just said about me. I want to set something straight with you. I have never, *ever* jumped into any man's arms the way I did into yours. I have never plotted and schemed to be with a man or to get him to kiss me, the way I did with you. I love you! I couldn't possibly be more committed to you than I am."

Rynn stared at her, stunned. "You can't...I... you're joking."

"I'm not joking."

"It's not possible. You've only known me a few days."

"You just told me you loved me! If you can fall in love in that short a time, why can't I?"

"I've seen a lot of life. I know what I want. I know how you make me feel, how alive I am around you. When you step from a dark room into the sunlight, believe me, you realize it!"

"Why am I incapable of recognizing the same sensation?"

"You can't be sure! You're so young."

"Do you think I achieved everything I have by being wishy-washy? I knew exactly what I wanted— and then I went out and got it! I'm not flighty; I'm very solid and down-to-earth. Granted, my family is a little flaky. But no matter how silly or vague or frivolous we may be, there's not one of us who doesn't know what he wants. Just try to take Elizabeth from her writing or Lionel from his toys. Ask Denise how easy it is to get Ken to abandon his goal. I'm not stupid. I'm not indecisive. I know what I want: you."

Impulsively Maressa sprang to her feet and strode over to him. Her hands went up to curve around his angular jaw and cheeks. She stood on tiptoe to brush her lips against his, and she felt the involuntary jerk of his body. Her tongue crept out and traced the firm line of his mouth. The temperature of Rynn's skin beneath her fingers soared.

"Maressa, please. You don't know what you do to me. This is cruel."

"Cruel?" she mocked and gently teased his lower lip between her teeth. "Then let me make up for my bad behavior."

His breath turned harsh and rasping as she pressed her body up into his and kissed him. Her tongue entered his mouth and he groaned. Suddenly his arms were around her, pressing her fiercely against him, his mouth devouring hers. His tongue was hot and flickering; his fingers dug into the soft flesh of her buttocks. "You're using me," he panted as he rained hot kisses over her face. "You're using my desire and love for you to get what you want." He nuzzled her neck.

Maressa chuckled deep in her throat and traced the whorls of his ear with her tongue. "I can think of better ways to use you," she told him huskily. "Would you like to see how I could use you?"

Rynn nipped at the lobe of her ear. He slid his hands up her body to her breasts, exploring every inch of flesh along the way, delighting in her response to his touch. His mouth ground against hers, taking, begging, giving. Maressa clung to him. "Rynn, oh, Rynn, I love you so much."

Suddenly he jerked away, whirling and striding off. He shoved his hands through his hair. "Maressa, if only that was all there was to it!"

"What do you mean?" she cried, hurt and angered by his rejection.

He turned, crossing his arms tightly across his chest. "God knows, I want you. It almost kills me not to touch you. But that's not all there is to love. I feel so much more than desire for you. I want to hold you forever, but I know I can't. You're here now, but soon you'd be gone."

Maressa seethed with fury; she realized she would have liked to punch him. "You know what your problem is? You don't have any trust. You say you love me, but you don't believe me. I've told you every way I know how that I love you. I want to marry you, live with you, have your children. I know what I want, and I'm willing to do whatever it takes to make it work. But you—you're plain scared. Afraid to give your heart, afraid to feel. You loved once before, didn't you, and went through hell because of it? It could happen again." Maressa drew a shaky breath. "Well, I can't swear I won't get sick or die. But I can promise I'll live every minute of every day until I die, and I'll love you all that time, too." She paused for a moment, looking at him, her head high, cheeks flaming with color. "If you don't want my love enough to risk the pain, then I guess I'll have to live with it. Goodbye, Rynn. Run on back to Atlanta."

Maressa swung on her heel and marched out the door, fueled by her rage and searing pain. She strode across the patio, her steps quickening until she was running, her eyes flooding with tears. She flung open the door to her house and ran inside, swinging the door shut behind her with all her strength.

But before it could close, the door was knocked back open with a blow that threatened to take it from its hinges. Maressa whirled on an intake of breath. Rynn filled the doorway, his form silhouetted ominously against the light. He paused for a split second and Maressa lifted her chin pugnaciously. He stepped inside, shutting the door softly. She could see his face now. His gray eyes brimmed with laughter and other, fiercer emotions. His straight mouth curved into a grin. "Don't you even give a guy a chance to admit he's wrong?" he asked. He shook his head in mock amazement. "How could I have ever thought you might not know your own mind?"

Maressa's mouth curved invitingly. "I can't imagine."

He came closer, reaching out to put his hands on her shoulders. Lightly he stroked her arms, letting his fingers glide down, then back up. Her skin prickled where he grazed it. "Maybe you were right and I was scared. Or maybe I was trying to retain some grasp on logic and reasonableness. Whatever it was, when I saw you walk out that door away from me, I knew I couldn't let you go. I couldn't live without you, no matter how unlikely or how frightening our love is. Nothing that I have is any good if I don't have you. I love you, Maressa. I love you more than anything in the world."

"And I love you." She gazed up at him solemnly, their eyes promising a lifetime of love.

He bent and kissed her. It was a seal, a promise given and received, a pledge of love. But with their mouths upon each other, their bodies close together, their kiss soon deepened. Rynn's mouth was hot and beckoning, seducing her even as it demanded her

response. Maressa's hands stole into his hair, combing through the thick dark strands, curling it around
her fingers and pulling him even closer to her.

"Love me," Rynn murmured thickly. "Love me."

Maressa tugged his shirt from his trousers and ran
her hands beneath it, tracing delicate designs on his
skin with her nails. Rynn pulled her more closely
against him, moving his hips suggestively on hers,
demonstrating how much his passion was already
aroused. Maressa moved her hands to his back and
down, slipping beneath the waistband of his trousers and onto his flat, muscular buttocks. He sucked
in his breath and leaned his forehead against the top
of her head. He nuzzled her hair for a moment, then
stepped back and impatiently unbuttoned his shirt.

Maressa began undoing his trousers, but as her
hands moved over the taut cloth, it was questionable
whether she was helping him to undress or simply
stoking the fire of his arousal. Finally Rynn set her
hands aside and feverishly ripped off his trousers
and underwear. Shoes and socks quickly joined the
pile, and he was naked before her. Maressa's eyes
drifted slowly down his body, admiring the hard,
blatant masculinity of his muscled form. "Don't just
look," he rasped.

Maressa glanced up at him, eyes shining, and
smiled teasingly. "I was trying to decide where to
start." She reached up and ran her hands down the
length of his arms and back up the soft inner side.
Her fingers slipped over his chest and back, caressed
his hips, and continued onto his hair-roughened
legs. She touched every inch of him, sliding down to

the floor and caressing the tender skin of his upper foot.

By the time she finished, Rynn was trembling from the effort of keeping his passion in check. He grasped her shoulders roughly and pulled her up to face him, then set to work undoing her clothes. He then proceeded to do to her what she had just done to him until Maressa was writhing, lost in an ecstasy of pleasure.

Desire was a live, wild thing within her, and no one could satisfy it but Rynn. His mouth aroused her past all reason. She twisted her head helplessly, moaning, and nipped at his bare shoulder. He shuddered, his arms tightening convulsively around her. Then, sweeping her off her feet, he carried her over to the bed in the room beyond. He set her down across the coverlet and stood looking at her for a long moment. Just the touch of his hot gaze increased the fever in her blood, and Maressa moved restlessly.

"Rynn," she breathed, and he lay down on the bed, covering her with his strength. Supporting his weight on his forearms, he moved up and down her body slowly, grazing her nipples with the hair-roughened skin of his chest.

At last he thrust into her, moving slowly and savoring each tormenting, delightful moment. Maressa moved with him, rotating her hips, surging up to meet him, and her movements sent his desire spiraling even higher. They moved to the wild, primitive rhythms of love, surging together to a shattering, glorious cataclysm. Pleasure poured through Maressa in waves, sweeping out to the extremities of her body and leaving her utterly, blissfully languid.

Rynn collapsed upon her, and Maressa wrapped her arms around him, holding him tightly against her. "I love you," she whispered.

"And I love you." He nuzzled her hair and kissed her ear. Reluctantly he shifted his weight from her and just as reluctantly Maressa released him. Rynn turned over onto his back beside her and stretched out his arms. Maressa nestled comfortably against him. A faint smile played across his lips. "To think I'll have this the rest of our lives—it seems too beautiful to be real."

"Oh, it's real, all right." She kissed his chest playfully. "Just try getting rid of me."

"Not likely." Rynn squeezed her tightly against him, then released her. "I can't think of anything more wonderful than going to sleep beside you each night and waking up next to you in the morning. It's like somebody has painted a rainbow across my life."

He yawned, stretching his jaw so wide it seemed it would crack. "Tired?" she teased.

He grinned. "I'll live. Although I may have to start taking vitamins to keep up with you." He yawned again. "I stayed up half the night talking to Denise or, rather, listening to her. What a night! I could live without another one like that for the rest of my life. When I checked in, the desk clerk gave me a leering grin—I mean, there I was with a nineteen-year-old girl and no luggage."

Maressa giggled. "Retribution for your checking in so easily with me yesterday afternoon."

"When we went upstairs, Denise began talking about Ken. I had to listen; I've wanted her to open up to me for years. But all the time I kept thinking about you and what I was going to do. The idea of leaving you tore my heart out, but I couldn't believe you loved me. I told myself that I had to leave for my own good, that if I kept flying back to Tucson to see you, I'd only prolong my agony. But my heart wouldn't listen to reason. It kept telling me all the reasons why I had to see you again."

"Good. I'm glad somebody was on my side."

"Even after Denise calmed down and went to bed, I couldn't sleep for thinking about you."

"Sorry." She raised up on her elbow and smiled down at him, her eyes dancing.

"You aren't, either. Not a bit." Rynn pulled her back down and kissed her soundly.

Idly Maressa twined several hairs on his chest around her finger. "Well, you can sleep all you want now."

"Not if you keep doing that," he growled, and she giggled. "You know what?"

"What?"

"I think I'll give Denise a little present. Just to take her mind off her woes. I'll send her on a Caribbean cruise for a couple of weeks before she starts her job at home."

"That ought to perk up her spirits."

"It'll also keep her out of the house the first two weeks of our marriage."

"What?" Maressa sat up excitedly. "We're getting married?"

"Of course. You didn't think I was talking about an affair, did you? I said I wanted commitment."

"Yes, but, so soon? Don't you want to wait a few months and be sure?"

Rynn grinned. "Didn't I tell you? I've given up being cautious. I want you in my life, in my bed, in everything I do, and I don't intend to wait a minute longer than I have to."

"Don't I have anything to say in the matter?"

"Of course. You can say yes."

"Yes."

"Good." He leaned over and kissed her, his mouth leisurely and arousing. Maressa's pulse picked up its beat, and she felt the heat of his skin increase against hers. At last he pulled his mouth away and, still leaning over her, gazed into her eyes. "Well, shall we go tell your parents there's going to be a Scott marrying a Taylor, after all?"

A slow, tempting smile curved Maressa's lips. "Later," she murmured and pulled his head down to hers. "Later."

ANNE MATHER

Anne Mather, one of Harlequin's leading romance authors, has published more than 100 million copies worldwide, including **Wild Concerto,** a *New York Times* best-seller.

Catherine Loring was an innocent in a South American country beset by civil war. Doctor Armand Alvares was arrogant yet compassionate. They could not ignore the flame of love igniting within them...whatever the cost.

HIDDEN IN THE FLAME

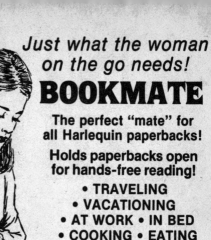
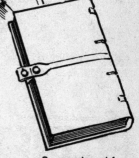